LOCKED

AND

LOADED

St. Martin's Paperbacks Titles by
ALEXIS GRANT

Sizzle and Burn
Locked and Loaded

ANTHOLOGY

Men of Danger

LOCKED
AND
LOADED

ALEXIS GRANT

St. Martin's Paperbacks

This is a work of fiction. All of the characters, organizations, and events portrayed in this novel are either products of the author's imagination or are used fictitiously.

LOCKED AND LOADED

Copyright © 2012 by Alexis Grant.

For information address St. Martin's Press, 175 Fifth Avenue, New York, NY 10010.

ISBN: 978-0-312-94304-2

Printed in the United States of America

St. Martin's Paperbacks edition / January 2012

St. Martin's Paperbacks are published by St. Martin's Press, 175 Fifth Avenue, New York, NY 10010.

10 9 8 7 6 5 4 3 2 1

PROLOGUE

Miami, Florida, Present Day

Sage stood under the intense, multihead shower spray, scrubbing her body with expensive shower gel until her skin felt raw. She'd definitely crossed the line. Other DEA Special Agents had warned her that it always came down to this when working on a long, involved undercover investigation. They'd told her to "get her head right" and to be ready, because there'd always be a point of no return when you had to decide how much of yourself you were willing to give for your country, willing to do to fit into the dark and decadent underbelly of illegal drugs.

The men who had preceded her on the case had gone in as deal makers, distributors, security forces, all in an attempt to trick Roberto Salazar into giving them access to his inner workings. But Salazar was no fool and each attempt by agents before her had gotten them close, but never close enough . . . until she'd entered the scene.

Before this assignment, she'd thought she could handle it. She didn't think she had a line. Her Field Division Supervisor kept asking her if she was prepared, and she'd repeatedly told him yes without blinking or stuttering. She'd wanted this. She'd hounded Hank Wilson until he'd given her the plum assignment. Drug kingpins from the infamous Salazar Brothers Alliance had created the chain of events that had left her mother and younger brother, along with her baby sister, dead—mowed down by ricocheted bullets in a territorial dispute. She had more at stake in this than anyone in the department. It was her trump card that finally got Hank to relent.

Innocents had bled to death in front of a corner grocery store. The Salazars' careless bullets had left her grandmother wailing in a hospital, on her knees in prayer begging doctors to revive DOA incoming. These same ruthless killers had left her grandmother stranded by grief in church, screaming over caskets . . . and had left her traumatized and mute when authorities collected her from North Miami High School to tell that, save for her Nana, everyone in her immediate family was dead.

Yeah, she'd lobbied for the assignment.

With her eyes closed, Sage turned off the water

with an unsteady grip, wondering how her life had become so completely screwed up by thirty years old. None of this was in her personal plan. She reached for a thick, Turkish bath sheet and pressed her face into the fragrant nap of the towel, remembering how she thought she could change things the second she'd graduated from Miami U with a BS in Criminal Justice, determined to be a part of the war on drugs. That seemed so far away now.

Sage let out a sad sigh and began drying off her body. Back then, women new to law enforcement held up Michele Leonhart as the consummate role model. Even to this day, she still was. Coincidentally, she had just been appointed to the DEA's Senior Executive Service to spearhead Special Agent Recruitment efforts at DEA Headquarters the same year Sage's family had been killed, 1996. Leonhart had broken through the glass ceiling and she was a woman who had it all . . . two kids, a husband, and a successful career in law enforcement. Sage's idol was a woman who'd worked her way up in the agency from a beat cop in Minnesota to finally be unanimously confirmed as the deputy administrator of the DEA by the US Senate. Leonhart was everything that she had once wanted to be.

But Sage was now pretty sure that her idol didn't own the dark need for vengeance that she did, and probably hadn't gone fully undercover to this degree. Although she didn't know for sure, she was fairly certain that Leonhart had stayed on the cleaner side of investigations.

Not looking in the foggy wall-to-ceiling mirrors, Sage walked over to the large, white marble sink and pumped body lotion into her hand. Nana had warned that unless she released her hatred of those who had killed her momma and siblings, one day it would destroy her soul. She used to scoff at that warning, unable to explain to her grandmother that more than revenge fueled her ambition. Fear ruled it.

It was impossible to just sit idly by and watch what had happened to her happen to other families. Her worst nightmares had come true as she witnessed the rising statistics of drug-related violence. Men like Roberto Salazar were getting stronger, not weaker. More families than ever before were grieving over innocent blood spilled. Being paralyzed by the threat of retaliation was more than her soul could bear . . . It was an ongoing violation of her spirit until the day she decided that, if she wasn't a part of the solution, she was part of the problem. Someone had to address the tide of destruction that had become a national tsunami. Given that she had nothing left to lose other than her life, who better to get involved?

When her Nana quoted scripture to dissuade her, Sage would remind her that somewhere it had said an eye for an eye and a tooth for a tooth. Nana never understood the full extent of her rage. It started off as very focused on her own personal pain and then as time went on and story after sad story in her community accumulated, the rage blossomed. Sage sighed again and applied more lotion.

Anger had been productive. Sage applied mineral-based anti-aging cream to her cheeks in gentle strokes. The powerful emotion had fueled her through college to graduate at the top of her class, and had rocketed her through the grueling requirements of the Police Academy. Rage and determination got her through the insanely competitive process of becoming a Special Agent, got her through sixteen intense weeks of training at Quantico. But maybe her Nana had been right, God rest her soul.

Sage stared in the mirror for a moment, glad that it was still opaque, and then twisted her long mass of freshly shampooed hair up into a mound on her head and clipped it in place.

Every one of her colleagues drew the line at killing an innocent human being to prove one's allegiance to the criminal they were trailing, but sleeping with the enemy or getting high with a target was par for the course. Blending in was para-

mount for survival. Her fellow veteran agents
had said that until she'd been initiated, truly experienced the gut-wrenching decision of total im-
mersion into that world, she hadn't really gone
undercover.

She'd definitely been initiated these last few
months. Right now she was way undercover,
bordering on being in too deep. Never had she
imagined that she'd have to go this far to exact
the kind of justice her soul demanded. But there
was no use in dwelling on it. Maybe she didn't
have a soul anymore. She wasn't sure if it had
fled her the day they'd told her that her family
had been slain.

The one thing she was certain of, however,
was that Roberto Salazar was about to do a mega-
deal with Anwar Assad. The Miami drug alliance was about to bring in major weight from
Afghanistan. A link with Al Qaeda was firmly
established due to her expertly placed bugs; getting close to Salazar gave her free access to the
ten-thousand-square-foot mansion, Salazar's marina, as well as the seventy-seven thousand square
feet of opulently manicured, waterfront grounds
that surrounded his Miami compound.

Now her Field Division knew for sure that
drugs flowing through Miami via a newly expected shipment were going to fund a large arms
buy—weapons from a Canadian source to be
used against US troops. The DEA's foreign-

deployed Advisory and Support Teams had echoed that intel. Her objective now that she'd gotten in close with Salazar was to find where the drop would take place, where the money was going to be wired, and who the Canadian arms contact was so they could catch the bastards.

Sage stared in the mirror full-on now, watching the steam slowly dissipate. Hell, yeah, putting her body on the line was worth it. Others had taken shrapnel or a bullet or a roadside bomb. She looked at her blurry image without blinking. Yes, she could continue this mission through to the bitter end, no matter what it took . . . not only for her family and for all those grieving families who had been caught in the crosshairs of drug violence, but for every person—military or civilian—who had been slain by terrorism.

"Small price to pay," she murmured and then turned away from the mirror to gather her sunscreen. Everything about her life now was a lie and the lines between who she'd been and who she was were as blurry as the bathroom mirror.

So what, that in order to get in, she'd had to play the role of Salazar's lover. It didn't matter that the moment when she'd been accepted into her target's inner circle and into his heart, she'd been forced to mentally separate from herself. If she was to be Salazar's woman, then she had to sleep with him. Period. But it wasn't her; the new identity took over. It was the only way she

could do what she'd had to do. Special Agent
Sage Wagner was now completely Camille Rodriguez, a biracial Latina . . . part African American and Latino, lover and numero uno girlfriend
of Roberto Salazar. She'd use whatever it took to
get in close to complete her mission.

She looked up calmly as the bathroom door
opened, tucking away her innermost thoughts. A
cool shaft of air rushed in with Roberto, sunlight
framing his six-foot-two, athletic build. He had
on a classic business suit; navy blue pinstriped,
single-breasted, Armani with a French blue, white-
collared shirt, paisley silk tie, and seeming quite
the dignified businessman. He was on his way
to Miami International Airport to meet with
Assad . . . but where were they headed after that?

"I thought you were going to wash yourself
down the drain?" Roberto beamed at her and
openly appraised her towel-clad form.

She tilted her head and offered him a pout.
"No, just getting ready to go shopping . . . are you
still going to your meeting alone or can you take
me this time? I can read a magazine or amuse myself in the cafés or shops wherever you're going
for a couple of hours until you're finished. Come
on, Roberto. I'm bored. After you're done, we
could do something fun."

"It has been a while since we've done something fun," he murmured, his eyes stripping away

the towel. "I admit that I've been preoccupied with business lately ... but it won't always be this way."

"After your meeting, we could go out ... or ... not."

She offered him a sexy half-smile and waited. When he hesitated and didn't immediately respond she moved toward him slowly, studying his handsome smile and intense, dark eyes, allowing his freshly barbered hair to thread through her fingers once she'd reached him. It had been several weeks since he'd touched her; the negotiations were obviously taking a toll on his libido—which was a good thing and a bad thing. Much could be extricated from him if he was still interested in her, a lot could be learned in pillow talk or when he spoke to his colleagues on the phone while in the bedroom. But lately he'd been aloof, and that wasn't good.

She leaned up and into him to brush his mouth with a kiss. "You took too long to answer me, so I already know the answer."

He circled her waist with his hands, caressing it through the damp towel. "I took too long to answer you because I was deciding, Corazón. You make it hard for a man to think about business." He kissed her deeply and then drew away. "But to keep you in fashion and in this mansion, there are certain things I cannot neglect ... *sí*?"

Hating that he'd tied her to his illicit deals, even if it was through the temporarily lavish lifestyle he shared with her or whatever other fantasy he'd concocted in his mind, she nodded and released a long, faux-submissive sigh. *"Sí."*

Fort Bragg, North Carolina

Captain Anthony Davis sat transfixed as his battalion commander gave his unit the briefing. The next generation of Salazar drug traffickers was expanding well beyond their Miami operations, making alliances with Afghan and Pakistan nationals that had known ties to both the Taliban and Al Qaeda. Satellite photos of the Salazar compound flashed across the briefing room screen.

"We've got seventy-seven thousand square feet exposed with a hundred-and-eighty-degree view of the water. This place was arrogantly built for luxury, not built to withstand a fast, preemptive strike," Colonel Mitchell said looking around the small DELTA Force unit. "Cabanas, pool, tennis courts, marina . . . all make good access points and hiding places, but don't get sloppy. Make no mistake, this compound is heavily armed, even though it seems fairly spread out and easy to wire. If the targets fall back to this position—which hopefully they will, with all of Assad's people—

I'd rather you go in and take them down the old-fashioned way, rather than leave a smoking black hole in this otherwise upscale, residential neighborhood. The main house is a ten-thousand-square-foot, seven-bedroom, seven-bathroom monstrosity that will leave quite an eyesore if you have to blow it."

"No trouble with the Posse Commitatus Act, Colonel?" Captain Davis asked carefully, and then glanced at Lieutenants Butcher and Hayes.

"No," Colonel Mitchell said in a flat tone. "We are in hot pursuit from our units in Afghanistan. That voids our concern about getting caught in a jurisdictional battle with the Drug Enforcement Agency or any other stateside law enforcement organization. We have word from the DEA through our International Joint Task Force on Homeland Security that the same target we have, Anwar Assad, is doing a deal in DEA's Miami jurisdiction. We are getting more intel as we speak from their field division special agents, and we're eventually going to need to establish a liaison relationship between us and the DEA. But right now, we're burning daylight. You better than anyone know that we cannot waste time with bureaucratic bull. We have to strike while the iron is hot. So, although our roles somewhat overlap on this one, our mission is clear."

The colonel began slowly pacing at the front of the briefing room, ticking off the points on his thick fingers as he enumerated them for his men. "One—confiscate the shipment to keep that insane amount of narcotics off our American streets; two—via Central Intelligence, our forces are to track all funds transfers so we can cast a wider net to catch even bigger fish, and so we can interrupt the cash flow of this operation to cripple it; and three—capture the bastards for future intel if we can, or exterminate them onsite if we can't. Allowing any of them to disappear back into the shadows or to hide behind the facade of being legitimate businessmen isn't an option. They're attempting to bring the party to our house, so, gentlemen, let's show 'em a real good time."

"Roger that," Captain Davis replied, staring at the beautiful woman who had briefly graced the screen. "How much civilian collateral damage is at risk within the compound, sir?"

"We're not sure at this time, because the household population changes daily based on whoever is visiting. That's why it's an option of last resort, but one that may ultimately be necessary—so rig it." Colonel Mitchell clasped his hands behind his back and lifted his chin, but his eyes were troubled. "There may be a few girlfriends and nonsecurity civilian staff inside the compound when the time comes . . . which is regrettable and also why I'm giving you orders to rig it for detonation as a last resort, but to preferably go in as a small, swift-moving assassin squad. It's always unfortunate to have civilian losses, but sometimes it's unavoidable."

"Understood, sir," Captain Davis said, glancing at his lieutenants, who nodded; he returned his attention to the colonel.

Although he outwardly seemed engaged in the colonel's words, in truth he was momentarily unable to get the image of the shapely, bikini-clad, cocoa-skinned woman with a million-dollar smile out of his head. He oddly found himself wondering what her eyes looked like behind the huge, black designer sunglasses she wore, and wanted to know how a woman who appeared so classy could wind up sleeping with a drug kingpin.

But just as immediately as the thought flitted through his mind, he banished it. Women like that did anything for money, and that same beauty would be the first one to put a bullet in his skull if she thought he was going to try to capture or kill her lover.

A long deployment in Afghanistan without regular female companionship was probably what was wearing on him, if he'd gotten temporarily distracted by a mere photo. Would have been nice to get one more quick trip in to Amsterdam for some paid brothel talent before he'd had to track Assad, but that was the last thing he needed to be thinking about at the moment.

Anthony immediately admonished himself. He was stateside now, just had to complete this mission, then he'd be able to have a life for a couple of weeks.

CHAPTER 1

Although the grounds seemed to be wide open and vulnerable, he knew better. Intel from the cell phone chatter and closer satellite feeds told him the place was crawling with guards and attack dogs, sweeping security cameras, and laser alarm fencing around the water side of the property.

But with a little creativity, it was possible to get in anywhere.

Using the pleasure boat traffic as a cover, Anthony silently slipped into the water and waited. Lieutenant Butcher was making an approach at the front of the house. As soon as the guards left the yacht that was moored on Salazar's dock, he could rig it and the two security speedboats with explosives, board the main vessel, quickly upload a viral image to their security camera software, then cover the grounds in less than seven minutes to strategically plant C4, and be out.

Anthony looked at his watch and stayed low behind his small moored fishing craft. As soon as he heard shouting and saw a huge, blond, bouncer-like guard stand up in the yacht's pilothouse, he moved in.

"Don't shoot the fucking dogs!" the blond guard shouted, coming out to assess the problem. "Are you stupid? You wanna draw cops here because a neighbor heard something? What did Roberto tell you?"

From the edge of the water beneath the dock, Anthony watched guards scramble to fan out with guard dogs pulling them forward.

"Pop the chains!" a burly Latino guard shouted. "It's not our fault if the mutts crossed the property line!"

Anthony packed C4 under the dock and slipped out of the water. Chaos was his cover. The alarms were already going berserk. A fence breach would be blamed for his diversion. By now, porn should have been showing up on the security cameras in the house as well as the boat; wireless networks were a bitch to secure and his people were the best at hacking in. Some poor bastard in Salazar's camp was going to take the fall for it, but who cared?

Laughter rang out along with booming curses. That's how he knew his strategy had worked. It was an insane one, but one the older vets had told him killed a lot of good men in WWII. Starving stray dogs were cheap and expendable. In that war, the enemy wired the animals with explosives and trained them to run under tanks to get fed, then *kaboom*.

His strategy this afternoon was a somewhat subtler approach. It was a known fact that male guard dogs could be trained to resist anything except a female in heat. Release four or five strays in heat on a compound, and you no longer had an effective pack of male guard dogs to contend with.

Up and out of the water in seconds, Anthony peeled off his black wet suit like a viper shedding his skin, then began running as if he were an animal control officer who had scaled the border property fence. In his peripheral vision, he could see Lieutenant Butcher dashing across a section of landscaped lawn with four henchmen running after their out-of-control Dobermans.

"We ought to shoot you for letting them get out of your truck," one henchman yelled out.

The blond in charge raked his fingers through his hair as one of the guard dogs that had mounted a female snarled at him when he approached it.

"I'm sorry, man," Lieutenant Butcher called out, purposely allowing a skinny female dog to dodge him. "Why don't you just let him finish, bro . . . like, it won't be that long, then I won't have to trank him so you can get him get back on a leash."

"Fine!" the blond yelled. "But you get this bullshit off our grounds pronto!"

"Done," Butcher said, trying to tuck away a smile as all five guard dogs became adhered in ecstasy to the strays, totally ignoring their primary job functions. "My partner went over the back wall to be sure there's no more running loose on the property, sir. He's got a van patrolling the area on an assist. So don't get trigger-happy if you see a tall black guy in a beige uniform, dude. We'll be out of here as soon as the Dobermans dismount."

The ruse worked. Several of the guards laughed, making lewd comments about female anatomy, but all seemed generally sympathetic to the temporarily powerless state of their attack dogs. Butcher had played his role beautifully, as if he was going for an Academy Award, even down to showing the guards how the lack of county funding had left his vehicle cage locks half-busted and unreliable.

The lieutenant's claim was that they'd gotten a local call about a small gator, and he and his partner's trucks were the only ones nearby in this area that had room in them at the moment. A speed bump on the cul de sac had jarred everything loose—that, along with eager female canines pushing on the doors after clearly smelling male dogs in the vicinity, was the culprit.

Now he had to play his role, and thanks to Butcher, even if he was spotted, he wouldn't cause immediate suspicion. Dogs had been disabled. Cameras were on the blink. Guards and garage staff were in the front of the main building trying to get their animals back under control. Five minutes was all he needed to conceal C4 bricks wired with cell-phone detonators in the pool cabana, at the house foundation, and under the cars in the garage. In a matter of minutes, Plan B would be in full effect. Lieutenant Hayes was on airport detail, already tailing Salazar and Assad, gathering more intel to execute Plan A.

As he set down the last explosive, hiding it behind a drainpipe, Anthony looked up from the back west wall of the house as the unmistakable click of a gun hammer cocking pierced his right ear. Instinct made him immediately throw a hard elbow jab backward to catch the would-be shooter in his Adam's apple. But this assailant was shorter than he'd judged, didn't have an Adam's apple, and deftly moved away, anticipating the jab as though an expert in martial arts. The blow never fully connected, only grazed her cheek.

For a split second their eyes met, assassin to assassin. She was the beauty he'd seen in the briefing and now held a nine-millimeter on him. Her hard brown gaze told him that she'd seen him stash the explosive. They both knew she had no problem pulling the trigger, but he couldn't allow her to alert the guards.

Only two precious seconds had ticked by. In a flash he nodded forward with a powerful neck thrust to butt his forehead against hers and quickly deflected her right wrist to keep from getting shot. But she'd jerked her head back in a strong snap to avoid the collision, yet hadn't properly judged her own distance from the brick wall. Her skull slammed against the masonry with a crack and he could see it in her eyes that she was temporarily dazed when she tried to point her weapon at him again and needed both hands. He also knew that her uncertainty would make her more deadly. Once a person tasted fear or was wounded, they were more likely to do something erratic as panic set in.

Not giving her time to think or regain her balance, he moved in. Size and clarity were his advantage, but speed and adrenaline seemed to be hers. She rolled out of his attempted grasp and then delivered a gun butt blow to his temple that would have dropped him, if her aim had been a quarter inch better. But in the vastness of those frenetic fighting seconds, he could sense that she meant to capture him, not kill him.

She had a gun and yet hadn't fired it. If she were merely protecting herself and the property, she should have put a bullet in his skull at close range by now. After he'd reached for her and kept attempting to disarm her, she should have screamed. If this was a normal civilian . . . as a terrified girlfriend, she should have shot blindly and wildly—squeezing her eyes shut to pull the trigger, something to suggest that she was just a civvy. But she didn't. She was actually battling him in hand-to-hand freakin' combat, trying to apprehend him without alerting the guards? That had to mean she wanted information. This was a pro.

Then she made a miscalculation, a defensive move to match his aggression. She'd turned too slowly, her pivot being off by a hair, and his elbow jab caught her in the back of her skull. She went down hard, and he caught her before she hit the ground.

This was not a part of the plan. Who the hell was this woman?

If he left her body here, Salazar would be on high alert; the shipment might even be aborted and they'd lose months of surveillance work. Assad would slip back into the shadows. The entire mission would be in jeopardy; their targets would know that someone had gotten on the inside. If he left her in the grass with a gun in her hand, his lieutenant would probably be swiftly executed or worse—tortured for information.

Anthony peered up at the glass French double doors leading out to the patio where the female assassin had obviously emerged. A woman's purse was on the floor along with her high heels. She'd literally come to fight him Ninja style in her bare feet. Oh, no, this wasn't a civilian by any stretch of the imagination.

"Shit!" he murmured and then quickly ran across the patio, grabbed her purse and shoes, gathered her up in his arms, and began running toward the marina.

If he took one of the moored speedboats, it could be made to temporarily appear as though she'd gone out on the water. If she was missing from the house and no one saw her leave by car, his lieutenant wouldn't have time to get out of there.

He flipped her body, purse, and shoes into a boat and quickly covered her with a tarp, stashing her gun in the back of his Animal Control uniform pants. Snatching up his wet suit and goggles in a flash, he untied the boat and eased away from the marina. If she woke up before he got her secured, he'd have to chloroform her to keep her from screaming. Anthony felt for the small vial in his buttoned uniform pants pocket, relieved that it had survived the brief battle.

Nothing could be allowed to abort the mission, even if it meant that this mystery woman had to be detained to appear as though she'd left the house in a huff. After all, the guards had been talking shit about bitches and hoes and rudely speculating about which chica they would gladly do doggie style. Text messages could be sent to her lover from the cell phone in her designer purse for all he cared. But the next forty-eight hours were critical.

She woke up with a dull ache at the back of her head and a wicked case of nausea. Bright lights and oxygen tubes were an intrusion on her senses. Then as she slowly came around, pain snaked up from the back of her skull to the top of it, making her grab her head with both hands and squeeze her eyes shut.

"Easy, easy," a familiar male voice murmured. "You've got a concussion and took a dose of chloroform."

She instantly recognized her boss's voice and relaxed. "Did you get the name of that Mack truck or what, Hank?"

Sage slowly opened her eyes and then froze. The same guy who'd just tried to kill her was standing beside her boss?

"Captain Anthony Davis, let me introduce you to Special Agent Sage Wagner."

"My apologies, ma'am," the captain said in a solemn tone. "It wasn't until I made contact with my lieutenant that DELTA Force learned—after the fact—that DEA had an embedded agent in the Salazar compound."

Now she was pissed. Royally so. Even the need to puke wasn't going to keep her rebuttal in check.

Struggling to sit up, she ripped the oxygen tubes away from her nose. "You mean to tell me that you military guys just went into our setup, in our jurisdiction, and not only gave me a goddamned concussion and chloroformed me when I woke up in the boat, but possibly blew my cover?"

"Wagner, I don't think you should get up so quickly, and there's an explanation," her boss said as she swung her legs over the side of the bed, then winced.

"Do you know how long I've been working on this case? We are *this close* to nailing those bastards!" she said, her voice escalating for a moment until both the headache that yelling gave her, as well as her boss's glance toward the door, made her lower it. "Screw you, Captain. No offense. But bringing this guy down has been my life's work and you have no idea of what I've put on the line. Not a clue."

She winced again and glared at the man who'd possibly given her a permanent brain injury, but she was glad that he hadn't shoved her nose through her gray matter or broken her arm in two places to take her gun.

"Agent Wagner," the captain said in a contrite tone, "I am really, really sorry that neither of us was alerted prior to our stealth operation."

Sage rubbed the back of her head. "So this is what's known as friendly fire, I suppose?"

He didn't answer her question, but looked out

the window. "We were not given the intel that we needed at the onset. Information had to go through channels, and by the time it got to our unit, we were already locked and loaded. We're on the same team . . ."

"Like hell," she spat back, growing testier the more she thought about it. "Jurisdiction belongs to—"

"Stand down, Wagner," her boss said gently. "Posse Commitatus doesn't apply. They were in hot pursuit of Assad from Afghanistan, so they are within their rights to get involved. It just so happens that their target is doing a deal with our target, hence the overlap." Hank Wilson smoothed a thick palm over the bald section of his scalp. "I know how much this case means to you, Wagner. I do. I'm not taking you off of it, but I really don't know about you going back in there. We'll figure this out and no matter what, we aren't letting the Salazars walk."

Sage released a long, weary sigh and nodded. What else was there to say or do? Bureaucrats had again mucked up the works and had the left hand not knowing what the right hand was doing. She could have shot Captain Davis; he could have blown her up or snapped her neck like a twig. It made no sense. However, as irate as she was, she had to admit that they were both putting their lives on the line for a cause they deeply believed in, and were probably both victims of

bureaucratic stupidity. Hank was right. He usually was, and that annoyed her too at the moment.

"If you are up to it," the captain pressed on,
after a glance across the room at Sage's boss, "I
can give you a full briefing and would appreciate the same."

"Yeah . . . I bet you would," she said, still annoyed, but not knowing where to vent her frustration. "And I definitely want to know what you
guys have planned, since you've packed the
house foundation with C4. Anything else I need
to stay away from?"

"The marina. The yacht. The garage and all
vehicles."

She just stared at the captain. "Even the cute
little red Mercedes?"

He gave her a lopsided half-smile. It was a
nice smile, actually, and she offered him a grudg-
ing one in return.

"No, ma'am. It was obvious that the coupe
was yours . . . the pink-and-red heart dangling
from the keys that were hanging up in the garage
was a dead giveaway."

She chuckled even though it hurt.

"And that's the thing, Wagner," her boss said,
rubbing his palms down his meaty face. "It's too
dangerous for us to send one of my best agents
back in there. I was thinking remote surveillance
from this point. Plus, if they've gotta blow the—"

"Hold it," she said, about to stand up until she felt the cool breeze at the open back of her hospital gown. "I have to go back or Salazar will know something's wrong."

The DELTA Force captain nodded. "Affirmative, sir. It would be helpful if she made a call to Salazar and feigned disgust at what happened on the grounds of the compound today, citing that as the reason she fled by boat—not wanting to walk past the display of dogs to go get her car out of the garage. We've put it in a slip over in South Beach . . . I recovered her shoes and her purse. If she has a cell phone on her, she can call Salazar and sound completely offended by the lewd male commentary made by the guards—and trust me, sir, it was foul."

"The dogs were you guys?" she said, shaking her head and then wincing with a smile. "Oh . . . my . . . God. That was insane, but brilliant! And, yes, I heard some of that . . . it was indeed rude. I can make it work—I know Salazar. I'll throw a phone tantrum and make him send a car for me. All I have to do is be lunching at my favorite restaurant with shopping bags filling the seats, and I can fuss and tell him how horrified I was by the language . . . and seeing dogs humping in front of the mansion." She pressed a palm to her chest. "What would the neighbors say?"

"Thank you, ma'am," the captain said, and

kept his handsome smile respectful. But she could tell he really wanted to laugh.

She studied him in total now, noticing his massive, six-foot-four frame with appreciation rather than dread, since he was no longer an enemy combatant. He had a really nice smile, a solid, square jaw, and was handsome in a rugged, not pretty-boy, way. Black, short-cropped waves made his hair almost appear to be velvet and his intense dark eyes were rimmed with thick black lashes. His medium brown coloring and the hint of a very slight accent that she detected made his ethnicity hard to judge. He could have been Hispanic, African American, Dominican, or from any Caribbean island.

"Captain Anthony Davis, right?" she said, after a moment and then extended her hand to officially offer the olive branch of peace.

He nodded and shook her hand. "Also known as Juan Morales during this mission, if it goes beyond what we normally do."

"Aka Camille Rodriguez, back atcha, Captain." She raised an eyebrow. "What do you guys *normally* do?"

"Hard extractions of hostages or very straightforward target eliminations."

"Assassinations, essentially."

"Eliminations."

"Semantics," she said, folding her arms. "But I like it."

"It's what we do."

"For God and country."

"Yes, ma'am—for both."

"Cool."

Her boss smiled. "Well, since you guys didn't kill each other, how about if I get one of the fellas to bring up some coffee from the cafeteria for an in-room briefing while you get dressed?"

CHAPTER 2

"What the fuck happened?" Roberto Salazar spoke in a tense rumble as the head of his security team filled him in. He didn't have time for this bull. Assad's private jet would be taxiing in at any moment. "Find her and bring her home. Kill and dispose of any stray mongrels that are still on my grounds."

He clicked off his cell phone and stared out of the tinted limousine window. *Women.*

"What's wrong?" Hector asked nervously.

Roberto waved his hand. "Dogs got out of a county truck and ran on the property and it pissed off Camille, so she left."

"Dogs?" Hector said with a frown.

"*Sí*," Roberto replied, slowly finding amusement in the absurdity of the situation. "Bitches in heat."

"Are you serious? They called you for that?"

Hector slumped back against the leather seats and blotted his brow.

Then both brothers' eyes met and they burst out laughing.

"Oh, shit," Hector said, suddenly laughing so hard that he had to wipe his eyes.

"You're telling me?" Roberto shook his head. "I've got our whole empire riding on red and fucking mongrel dogs have invaded my house and my woman is having a fit about this? Madre de Dios, if this is the worst news I get today, then I'm a happy man."

Hector picked up the glass of aged Scotch that sat on the bar beside him and lifted it to Roberto. "If that is the worst of our worries, then we can definitely thank the Blessed Virgin." He knocked back the drink and ran his fingers through his hair. "The waiting is the worst part, no?"

"That is always the hardest part, Hector . . . that is the part of what we do that defines a man's cojones. So, have another drink, but don't get sloppy. When we meet Assad, I want you calm, confident . . . *comprende*?"

Hector nodded and poured a half a glass of the amber liquor. "You can count on me, Roberto."

"*Bueno*," Roberto murmured and then fell silent for a moment to stare out the limousine window at the planes taking off and landing. "You are sure about this arms contact you researched?"

"Absolutely. Charles Wallace is ex-Soviet and

has tentacles well positioned to deliver what Assad wants."

Roberto turned and stared at his brother. "I cannot oversee everything, Hector. The business is getting too big . . . I've taken care of my part—the product, our security forces, the distributors, and setting the terms of the deals. And that Assad also buys his arms from us at a reasonable rate so that he'll come back again and again. This way we'll always have cheap but pure product in our pipeline and they'll always have top-grade arms in theirs. As my brother, there is *no one* else I can trust with something like this. So you cannot fuck this up, Hector. The arms part has to be as airtight as the drug and money deliveries."

Hector gripped his glass and stared into Roberto's eyes. "I *know* what's at stake, and *I said* I have handled it. You have to start to have more faith in me, Roberto . . . to believe in me like I believe in you."

"You're right. I'm sorry," Roberto said after a moment and then looked out the window again. "I'm just used to controlling all the details, but as we expand, it is not possible . . . it's nerves talking."

Tense silence surrounded both men as they each retreated into their own thoughts. Fifteen minutes of waiting produced Anwar Assad's private charter coming in from Toronto. A sense of satisfaction and power threaded through Roberto's nervous system. Much could be accomplished when one knew the right people and which palms to grease. He did. Getting men on the inside of TSA was no different. Human nature always allowed for a variable. Roberto smiled as he tapped on the divider window and his driver got out.

His guard opened the door for him and his brother as they debarked the limo and walked swiftly to meet his Gulfstream III jet on the tarmac. As soon as the steps were lowered, Roberto and Hector swiftly ascended the stairs and entered the craft.

"Gentlemen, how was your flight?" Roberto said, looking around at the four serious faces of the men who were waiting.

"Very good," Assad said, offering Roberto a slight bow.

Roberto motioned with his arm for Assad and his men to sit as the plane began to taxi. "I take it all went well with Charles Wallace in Toronto?"

"Indeed," Assad replied with a cautious smile. "His name is Anglo, but he is an old Russian."

Roberto laughed and gave a glance of approval toward Hector, who preened from the silent compliment. "Easier to transfer funds to accounts that do not give rise to suspicions, true?"

Assad nodded.

"So . . . he showed you what you needed to

see at Boston's Technology Trade Show, and you were pleased?"

"I am very pleased," Assad said, glancing around at his men. "But my ultimate pleasure depends of Aalam Bashir feeling the same way."

"Of course, of course," Roberto said, waving his hand. "Trust, but verify."

Assad bowed slightly from his seat. "Trust, but verify."

"So, while I am trusting you and you are trusting me, and we are both waiting to verify our deliveries from one another, shall we spend the time in New Orleans enjoying the casino and the women?" Roberto smiled and motioned toward the male security guard doubling as a flight attendant to bring a bottle of Cristal to the group. "Oh come now, gentlemen," Roberto said when he saw them hesitate. "Tell me you are not of the rank that are looking to blow yourselves up and are saving yourselves for twenty-one virgins, are you?"

Assad's men cast nervous glances toward him, and Assad nodded his permission for them to accept the champagne flutes being offered.

"I do not believe that is our fate," Assad said with a sly half smile. "What a man does in private is between him and Allah."

Anthony stood outside Special Agent Sage Wagner's hospital room, listening to her boss drone on about their mutual targets of interest. His gut hunches rarely proved wrong, even in this case. When he'd first seen her on the screens while getting a mission briefing, she'd arrested his attention. It had been impossible to shake her presence out of his mind, but the way she'd been grouped with Salazar, it seemed like she was an enemy sympathizer—what else could he believe, especially when she'd pulled a gun on him? But by not listening to that nagging voice within, he'd almost done the unthinkable to one of his countrywomen. Damn.

Still quietly kicking himself, Anthony responded to Hank Wilson with crisp, perfunctory answers as both men waited for coffee to be brought up for the meeting they'd have once Sage was dressed.

As much as he hated to admit it, the entire concept of her literally being embedded with the enemy bothered him. Until now, it had never really crossed his mind how gender differences could affect the role of a female agent working undercover. There were no females in DELTA Force, at least not on the combat side of their operations. Those who were tertiary to the unit were in support roles in military intelligence or logistics. And yet this sharp, capable, gorgeous woman had put more on the line in service to her country than he'd ever had to consider.

It made him want to know more about her.

Who was this woman he'd almost killed? What could drive a woman of Special Agent Wagner's obvious talent to want to take on a role like this? Surely she had her choice of assignments; was blind ambition the ice water that ran through her veins?

"So, Captain, this is definitely a 'no guts, no glory' mission," Hank Wilson remarked and then waited.

Anthony wrested his attention back to the conversation. "Roger that. We want Assad alive, if possible. If not, we need to send his side a message. A very profound message, hence the C4 at the Salazar compound."

"Just don't toast my agent," Hank warned, losing some of the easy camaraderie that had been in his eyes. "Wagner is the best I've got, and if there's any way to work it out, I want her to get a piece of taking down the Salazars."

"I'm sure you understand that my unit can't worry about or guarantee jurisdictional credit or career enhancing—"

"It's not for that," Hank said quickly, cutting him off. He lowered his voice and stepped in closer. "For Wagner, this is personal. She's gonna go in, take risks that . . . well, just know that she'll die trying to bring down the Salazar drug empire."

For a moment Anthony just stared at Sage's boss. What had the Salazars done to this woman?

A silent understanding passed between both men. Hank's eyes held a plea, even though his expression was stern and his voice had never wavered. The depth of concern in Hank's unblinking gaze connected with something within Anthony that he couldn't name. Words were insufficient as both men clearly struggled with how to articulate what couldn't be asked or said.

To end the brief standoff, Anthony simply nodded. It was the best he could do, the best acceptance of Hank Wilson's terms he could offer under the circumstances.

"I'm decent," Sage announced, cracking the door open. "The dress is dirty, but hey."

Hank caught the edge of the door, cast another meaningful look in Anthony's direction, and then accepted two cups of coffee from an approaching agent. "Thanks, Dan."

"No problem."

Special Agent Dan Jennings handed a hot Styrofoam cup to Anthony as the three men entered the room. Anthony thanked him while monitoring the body language of both men before his eyes settled on Special Agent Wagner.

She'd been injured, she was in way too deep, and he'd potentially compromised her cover—but it was clear from her expression that she would not be deterred from attempting to go back in.

She had taken her lush mass of hair down from

its former long ponytail and was wearing that same wide gold belt and white micromini dress that he'd met her in, something that amounted to little more than a short tube of stretchy white fabric. It clung to every outrageous curve she owned as though it had been painted on her, and she still looked fantastic in it, even if it was slightly smudged from their combat and where he'd dumped her into the speedboat. She'd recovered her chunky gold bangles, necklace, and earrings from the plastic hospital bag, and was now leaning against the bed in gold stilettos that made her long, satiny legs appear to go on forever.

But she paid the men before her no mind as she focused on a small gold compact mirror she was holding and tried to blot makeup on over her arm bruises. He thought about the defensive moves she'd made, how her skillful blocks had kept him off balance, and was so glad now that she was an adept fighter. Yet, even blocking him, there was contact—hard male muscle against butter soft female skin, and it was going to leave a mark.

When she winced as she dabbed the compact pad beneath her left eye where he'd grazed her, Anthony inwardly cringed. If that blow had actually connected, it would have shattered her cheekbone and been ruinous to her gorgeous face. For the first time in his life, he thanked the good Lord that he'd sparred with an armed combatant who had almost bested him and had dodged almost every blow.

Even though she'd aggressively come at him, he'd never ever laid a hand on a woman before. All the training in the world hadn't prepared him for that. Then learning that she was a friendly, more than that—a fellow warrior—was going to jack with his head for a long time. Seeing the result of their hand-to-hand combat now made him sick to his stomach.

"Okay, here's the plan," she said, without missing a beat. "I need a lift over to South Beach— back of a van, blacked-out windows, whatever. Drop me off discreetly in a parking lot or something so I can go into one of my fav boutiques. I'll explain that I had a little domestic trouble if asked. Shopping all day will be my cover."

"Not before you get an MRI to be sure there's no bleeding on your brain or anything else," Hank warned in a no-nonsense tone. "I'm serious."

"Okay, but after that, I'm outta here. And can you tell 'em I have to do this stat, like none of that hanging out in a hospital gown in a hallway for five hours? I'm doing it in my clothes. Fast. Only because I love ya, Hank. But you and I both know that the longer I'm here, the harder it'll be to get back inside without a problem. If you really care about my health, you'll make sure

I can go back to Salazar without raising any suspicions."

"All right, all right, I'll see what I can do." Hank released a long, weary sigh and sipped his coffee. "You're gonna make me start smoking again, Wagner, I swear."

Sage winked at Hank and then held up the mirror again. She let out a huff of annoyance as she glimpsed her damaged manicure, and then the side of her jaw, and flung the compact on the bed with her purse. "I'll get a wardrobe change, and will come out of the front door of the boutique with enough bags to justify being AWOL for a couple of hours, and then head to a restaurant. I'll let Bruno find me there."

"And then go lie by the pool or something, Wagner . . . just take it easy for a day or so."

"In there? Take it easy?" She smiled at Hank, and it was a heart-stopper. "I'll do my best, boss. I promise."

"That's why I don't want you going back in." Hank frowned at her, which only made her gorgeous smile get wider.

"I'm going in, Hank," she said calmly. "I'll go lie by a pool and sip a margarita when all these bad guys are dead or behind bars."

Agent Jennings ran his fingers through his blond crew cut and looked at Anthony and then at Hank Wilson when Hank handed Sage a cup of coffee. Anthony kept his eyes on Sage. The dynamic was tense, but interesting.

"Do you really think this is advisable, Wagner? Dan can—"

"Hank, it's now or never. My cell phone has been blowing up with calls and text messages from Bruno, Salazar's head of security at the house. We're lucky that it took him a couple of hours before he even noticed I was missing. A boat being gone from the marina probably gave it away. But I just sent him a text back that told him to go screw himself after what I saw and heard on the grounds, so he knows I'm fine and thinks I took the boat now . . . and otherwise believes that I'm just being femininely pissy about the whole dog incident."

She smiled at Hank and accepted the coffee, but her smile didn't reach her eyes as she glanced at Anthony. "My biggest problem is going to be hiding the bruises. With my luck, Salazar will think I was with some guy who beat me . . . some type of sick lover's dispute or jealousy thing that happened because I'm out there two-timing him, and *that,* more than anything else, is enough to get me killed. But I'll think of something. I always do."

The room remained silent as Sage took the lid off her coffee and sipped it slowly. After a moment she looked up and captured Anthony's gaze within her own. "We had enough on Salazar to bring him and his brother in a month ago. But then I learned that he was trying to do a deal behind his Colombian supplier's back. Arturo Guzman isn't going to be happy when he finds out that our man Salazar cut himself a sweet deal with the Taliban dudes that have ties to Al Qaeda. Salazar isn't stupid, and he's been on edge ever since he brokered this new deal." Sage took another careful sip of her coffee as though considering each word as the strong black fluid washed over her tongue.

"A nervous man is a dangerous man," Anthony said, never breaking eye contact with her.

"Absolutely."

Tense silence threaded between them as she pushed off the side of the bed and sauntered to the window. "Here's the thing. Salazar is an ambitious sonofabitch, so he took the risk. Being wealthy isn't enough for him—he also wants power. Like government impacting power."

She turned and faced them, abandoning her coffee on the windowsill, then crossed her arms. "Salazar wants what Guzman has, the ability to attend state dinners and tell presidents and captains of industry how things are going to go. He ultimately wants his US empire to mirror those of his mentor and rivals. He doesn't want to wait for old man Guzman to bequeath power to him; Salazar wants to set his own terms and seize it now while he's a relatively young man."

"Pretty bold move and a good way to get himself wiped off the face of the map, if Guzman finds out," Anthony replied, staring at Sage. He hadn't meant his tone to sound like a challenge of her knowledge of the situation, but as soon as he'd finished the statement, he could tell from her body language that's how she'd processed it.

"I know this man *well*," she retorted, drawing herself up to stand taller. "He's gonna do the deal."

She allowed the simple reply to hang in the air, leaving no doubt that her insider knowledge as Salazar's lover went deeper than any surveillance could ever convey. Why that grated on him, he wasn't sure. But it did. And it made him temporarily stand down.

This much he knew: Men only talked about their dreams to a trusted female source, men disclosed to that woman what they would never disclose to another man, and only if that woman had become more than a body in bed. He'd been there and also knew how it cut to the bone to be betrayed, which was why he'd personally vowed to never go there again.

If Salazar had let Sage in that close, past all his criminal instinct and street smarts, Special Agent Sage Wagner was walking on a tightrope with no net. A betrayal of that level of trust for a man like Salazar was a death sentence for the woman who'd played him. Sage Wagner had to know that. Looking into her eyes, he could tell that she did.

Maybe it was sheer hubris or courage or a combination of both, but her steely grit told him that she didn't care. A nervous man was a dangerous man . . . but a fearless woman was lethal.

"So," Sage said, after waiting a beat to be sure there were no more challenges to her leadership on the case, "that means all of Salazar's drug capital will ultimately get converted into lucrative, legitimate holdings. I'm talking stocks, bonds, real estate, and manufacturing concerns, you name it . . . with sweetheart government contracts attached wherever he can get them for all his institutional-type business tentacles. The man has more accounts offshore than you can imagine, Captain, and even has his money in prison uniform manufacturing, institutional food processing plants, waste management, construction— he's no fool, not by a long shot. Dude is smooth; does the local Chamber of Commerce events in black tie and makes significant anonymous donations to the candidates of his choice. We are talking about someone who is positioning himself for greatness."

"He's come a long way from being a wild street punk doing drive-bys and turf wars. But this guy was smart—even as a kid. We could never directly pin anything on him or his brother. Anyone who might have talked always clammed up or

wound up dead before we could get a statement."
Hank Wilson glanced at the other agents, his
gaze lingering on Sage for a moment before he
resumed.

Anthony took a careful sip of his coffee, observing the DEA team. Hank Wilson was the
boss, but obviously worried out of his mind for
Sage—while at the same time trying not to treat
her like a daughter or usurp her rank in front
of an outsider. The kid, Dan, had a wide-open
crush on his mentor agent that she seemed oblivious to. Regardless of the interdepartmental poli-
tics, he had a job to do and the information they
were providing was invaluable.

"That's how they rose so fast in Guzman's
army. We've been tracking his deals through
Special Agent Wagner," Hank added with a nod
toward Anthony, taking a loud slurp of his coffee. "Her work has been phenomenal. Knowing
exactly where all of his holdings are will allow us
to seize it all once we drop the hammer. Then this
whole Assad wrinkle came on our radar and we
held off taking Salazar down, trying to see where
it led. It just keeps getting bigger. If the stars
align correctly on this one, Captain, for the first
time on US soil, we'll have a wholesaler who is
almost as wealthy as the main Colombian man-
ufacturer. All of the drug enforcement and law
enforcement agencies have a lot at stake here

on this one, Captain—no disrespect to DELTA Force."

Anthony nodded. "Understood, sir. We'll do what we can to not flush your traps, but we also have a job to do. We cannot allow a weapons deal to go down that will endanger our troops or harm American and ally citizens."

Sage lifted her chin, telegraphing a nonverbal thanks toward Hank for his support, but still clearly wary of the new variable in the game.

"Fine, Captain," she said, glaring at him. "Here's where the trip wires are. I want you to know, so you guys don't accidentally blow anything we're working on. Salazar has gone behind Guzman's back for a silent power grab. If Salazar gets pure product in from Assad at half the cost he has to pay Guzman for it, he's pulled a quiet, bloodless, financial coup—eliminating the middleman."

"And Assad needs cash fast to keep his terror cells in weapons all around the globe, so he's willing to sell cheap," Anthony said with a nod. "We've been trying to broker a buy as Colombians to get one of us in close to Assad, hence my alias—Juan Morales. But we never got in close enough to make the deal click. Then we found out about the connection between Assad and Salazar, and pursued it here. And you guys decided to bum-rush your way into Salazar's compound rather than finesse it." Sage shook her head and folded her arms again. "You could have blown the entire operation. Just like Intelligence does, we have *a lot* invested in this, Captain. A helluva lot."

"Then get me in your way so we can get a drop on when the shipment is going to go down—and so we can hit them before they even know what's happening," Anthony said, folding his arms. This woman disturbed him, down to the marrow of his bones. She was gorgeous, deadly, talented, and patriotic . . . an odd combination he'd never seen before now.

She shook her head, challenging him. "Not possible. Just—"

"We've got a man on the inside up in the Bronx, who's currently one of Salazar's top distributors," Dan Jennings offered. "Our guy, Agent Alvarez, has been working undercover doing the buys from Salazar. Maybe we can have him vouch for Captain Davis?" Dan glanced at Sage and then Hank before hurriedly pressing his point when her eyes narrowed. "Salazar is going to have to do a quick, surgical strike to turn over his new product and to get cash in for it so he can make his moves before Guzman catches on. Salazar's got a strong connection in New York who can get it through Canada. But if we take his guy out, he'll need help. Then all we'd have to do is get our embedded guy to say that Captain Davis, aka Juan Morales, is his new righthand man, and he's got the ties to get it up and out. It'll be one of our strongest plants yet."

If looks could kill, the glare Sage Wagner shot in Special Agent Dan Jennings's direction would have left him DOA. Anthony suppressed a smile.

"Whaduya say, Wagner?" Hank hedged. "If Salazar is making a huge buy from Assad, he's definitely gotta move the weight fast and get it shuffled into his pipeline before Guzman gets wise to it—especially if the cut quality goes up substantially. That means he's got to rally the distributors and get them to push it through their networks to flip it quick. We could use the extra boots on the ground to take out the distributors at the same time we bring down Salazar and his men."

"The only extraction *we* want is Assad and his men for future intel, and we have no problem doing what is necessary." Anthony said, staring at Sage.

"Do you really want to put these bastards behind bars?" Dan said, his voice straining with emotion. "Or do you want to have done what we can't really do under law enforcement . . . if DELTA Force is handling a terrorist threat, it's an act of war, right?"

Hank smoothed a palm over his bald spot as he looked between Sage, Dan, and Anthony. "Dan's got a point, Sage. How many times have you seen these kinds of guys wiggle out of sentencing or run their empires from behind bars? Besides, I wouldn't mind having an extra pair of eyes backing up my star agent while all this crap goes down . . . especially some guy from DELTA Force. I want you walking outta there in one piece, Wagner. It was bad enough that we were dealing with cutthroat Colombians. Now that we've got the Taliban and possibly Al Qaeda in the mix . . . sheesh."

Sage released a huff of frustration and kept a penetrating gaze on Anthony. "Fine. Whatever. But when this all goes down, I don't want to hear about a State Department deal or some other crap that allows Salazar and his brother to walk. I want the whole thing toppled and those two rat bastards either in prison or on a slab with tags on their toes—we clear?"

"Affirmative." Anthony lifted his chin, understanding her indignation about his involvement, even if he didn't particularly like it. "I think you saw that I was prepared to do the latter before the former."

Sage paused. "I'll give you that, Captain. Gotta admit that I like your style. C4 . . . not bad for a day's work; just make sure I'm not around when you detonate."

Her wry comment made him smile a slight half-smile, despite his resolve not to.

"Roger that, ma'am. But an extra guy to watch your six and to lock and load on a target is never viewed as a bad thing in my unit. I suspect the same would be true in yours, if we'd met under better circumstances."

"All right. Fine," Sage said in a tight, resigned tone. "We have a plan . . . you'll work your way in as a distributor via Special Agent Michael Alvarez's recommendation—you're his cousin. Maybe you'll be positioned to buy the lion's share of the product or something, so we can keep tabs on all that product, which we don't want out on the open market once this sting goes down. That will let you know when phase two is about to happen—phase one is the shipment; phase two is when Roberto has to flip it. Tell your commander, or whatever your reporting structure is, that you're going to have to have cash to flash. Suitcases of it in the millions. Not to mention some expensive clothes and a decent car, not too over the top since you're lower level, but enough to say you're doing all right."

Now he had a problem. He'd have to get word back, work through channels fast, and be ready. This was way beyond their standard operating protocols and fell more under the purview of law enforcement agencies or Intelligence. But as he stared at Special Agent Wagner, somehow going outside the dotted lines seemed worth it.

"We can do that for him," Dan said in a hesitant tone. "Alvarez can hook him up—we've got a lot of stash up in New York."

"Whatever." Just like that she abruptly turned away from him and looked at Dan hard. "Meanwhile, can a girl get a lift to South Beach? I've been gone long enough already."

Dan hesitated. "Sure."

Again, nervous glances passed between the two male DEA agents and Sage. It was clear that her boss didn't want to discuss the matter of DELTA Force involvement on their case any further; it was a done deal, which he'd no doubt have to argue about on a solo drive with Sage Wagner all the way to South Beach. Special Agent Jennings obviously didn't want to be alone in a vehicle with Special Agent Wagner to catch a ration of shit behind his helpful recommendations.

"I can do the drop-off," Anthony finally said, breaking the strained silence in the room. Keeping his focus on Sage, he spoke to the group. "I want to get inside Salazar's head. I need to understand the kinds of moves he might make so that we can anticipate what might transpire with him and Assad, to nail them both. Special Agent Wagner has the best psychological profile on one of my secondary targets. Since we're going to have to work together, now seems like the best time to develop as much of a rhythm as we can before we have to work for periods under a communication blackout."

All eyes were on Anthony now. He hoped that

Sage would accept the compliment he'd lobbed in her direction as the best olive branch he could offer at the moment. Her boss gave him a slight nod and then glanced at Sage as though waiting on her okay.

She nodded. "Makes sense, but I need some cooperation, Captain. I know we each report up through different nonintersecting channels, but if we don't communicate and keep each other informed, solo heroics could get one or both of us killed."

"I understand," he said, fully respecting where she was coming from. She was right. One false move, one misstep in behavior, and covers could be blown, and lives lost.

"Good," she said without ever losing eye contact with him. "Nice to know that this time you do."

CHAPTER 3

"Twenty-one," Roberto said, glancing down the table at his brother.

Hector closed his eyes and stood as a shapely blonde collected Roberto's chips. "I've had enough games."

"Then why don't you go check on our clients and make sure they're enjoying themselves?" Roberto allowed his palm to slide across the blonde's ass. "I know I am . . . you should too."

He stood and gave her several chips, putting the rest in Hector's hand. "Stop sulking."

The gift only seemed to make Hector's expression darken, but he couldn't worry about Hector's little tantrum right now. His brother had been like that since they were children; always hated losing but never aggressively pursued doing otherwise. Right now he wasn't going to let Hector piss him off. He'd been under enough stress.

"Want to go to your suite?" The blonde nuzzled his neck and then pulled back.

He smiled and put his arm around her waist and began walking. As they passed the VIP tables, he could see Assad and his men thoroughly engaged in the games. A dark thought slithered through him as he watched his brother head to the cashier's booth, rather than do what he'd been told—entertain their guests. Hector was such a spoiled little bitch that sometimes he literally hated him.

But the weeks of pure focus and his momentary vexation with his brother were becoming unraveled as he stepped into the elevator and the blonde's hand slid across his groin. For the first time in weeks he felt his desire stir as he thickened in her hand.

By the time they'd reached his top floor suite, he was ready for her. Glancing around the room to visually case it, he sat down on the sofa and pushed away the coffee table with his foot. She knew what to do. He didn't have to say it.

With a smile she knelt down and unzipped his pants as he leaned back and closed his eyes.

"*Gracias*," he murmured. "Swallow and watch the suit. I have to get back downstairs to a meeting soon."

With the logistics and communication protocols discussion out of the way, Sage sat in the back of

the unmarked black van staring at the clean barbered line at the nape of Captain Anthony Davis's strong neck. As he'd driven, they'd traded
safe words, hammered out rendezvous points,
and she now knew her profile would be uploaded
to Central Intelligence and Military Intelligence.

Everything was a shadowy silhouette as she
peered through a pair of dark designer sunglasses.
The windows of the van were almost totally
blacked out and the windshield was glare-tinted,
just like her life seemed to be. She could see out;
no one could see in. She couldn't remember when
she hadn't been on a mission to advance, to get
closer to her objective, and somewhere along the
way she'd forgotten to *live*.

Something about the man before her unsettled
her in a way that was impossible to define. For all
intents and purposes, he was her new partner—
another short-lived event that she could only
pray wouldn't end in tragedy.

Who the hell was this guy, though? *DELTA
Force*—the Universe obviously had jokes. But
just as soon as her mind latched on to trying to
figure out his backstory, she banished the temp-
tation of curiosity from her mind.

She didn't want to know anything about him,
really. Once you got to know about people, you
bonded with them, worried about them, and
cared too deeply if they lived or died. It had taken
everything within her to keep everybody on the

team—especially Dan Jennings, who had a crush on her—working the research and remote intel side of the job. She liked it better going in solo and hated having to worry about other people.

It had been a no-brainer to push Dan away—not for personal reasons, but so the rookie didn't get himself killed trying to be a hero, or get her killed by raising an eyebrow at the wrong place at the wrong time. She despised having to worry about a team member, and prior to Captain Davis's inelegant entry into her case, she'd had a clean span of control within a hostile environment. Now she had to worry about Captain Davis, even though it was clear that he could handle himself—he could still get shot if Salazar got nervous. That was the last thing she needed on her conscience.

Usually Hank understood things like this, but there was no pressure like Pentagon pressure—so what options did her boss have to keep DELTA Force from usurping her team's jurisdictional prerogative? None. However, that didn't mean she had to like it.

"So what did he do?"

Captain Davis's question jarred her out of her thoughts.

"Roberto Salazar's rap sheet of *alleged* activities—and I say alleged because we never caught the bastard redhanded in a way that we could make stick—is a story much longer than the drive to South Beach will take. Didn't they fill you in before you went loading C4 under the man's house?"

"They did, ma'am. But let me clarify the question. What did he do to *you*?"

Sage paused as Davis glanced up at his rear-view mirror.

"He threatened my American way of life. Same thing all bad guys do."

This time he turned and looked at her over his shoulder. "Not acceptable."

"Not acceptable?" Sage just stared at the man. Who the hell did he think he was?

"Absolutely not, if we are going in as a team to bring down an extremely dangerous target of interest. We have to work as a unit, be able to shadow each other and anticipate each other's moves when out of communication range or opportunity. That means I have to know what the stakes are for you."

"Aren't they obvious?" she said in a tight tone. "I've been working this case for a long time and have a lot invested in it. I want the Salazars put away and their empire of drug trafficking crippled—better yet, totally dismantled, if possible."

"Still not acceptable."

"What's that supposed to mean, Captain?"

"I mean, what's in it for you, personally?"

He waited. She didn't have an immediate response to give him. She'd only had this level of conversation with Hank, someone she'd known for years and trusted. She didn't know Captain Davis from a can of latex paint.

"All right," she said, releasing a long, impatient breath. "I know your ass is on the line, Captain, and I won't—"

"Both our asses are on the line, ma'am, if I may speak freely."

Sage took off her sunglasses and leaned forward as he entered the highway ramp. "Listen you arrogant, sarcastic—"

"I didn't mean that as a dig or a lewd reference. I am stating the facts and respect the hell out of what you've probably had to endure. But *the fact* is, if I step on your toes in there because I don't understand what your true, off-the-record objective is, then as the newcomer to the unit I could screw up fast. I'm trying to avoid that while also following my mission as stated by my chain of command. I also need to know if you're going to go rogue in there, and in an attempt to create your own brand of justice, do something on the fly that could put me and any other men in my unit that are on this mission at risk."

Sage eased back and stared out the window, reliving the painful memories that had brought her to this point in her life. She slowly put her sunglasses back on. In context, it was a fair question . . . but it was ironic that she'd be rehashing her past with a man who had kidnapped and tried to kill her only hours earlier.

"When I was in high school, my mother was walking into the local corner grocery store with my little sister and brother. They were home from school that day because they were both sick . . . she had to pick up some cough medicine. That's also why my grandmother wasn't watching them at her apartment so my mother could go to work. Nobody wanted Nana to possibly catch the flu, given her age. Roberto Salazar and his brother, Hector, were working their way up in the Guzman organization."

She let out a weary breath after a long pause, glad that Captain Davis didn't interrupt. "The Salazars were embroiled in a street turf battle and sprayed the corner where the Haitians were trying to sell. It wasn't about my mother, my baby sister and younger brother, the old man at the bus stop, or the grocer's son. It was just business. They all died. Everybody in the hood knew who did it and some even saw it. But no one would step forward to testify. I couldn't blame them. *Don't snitch* isn't about loyalty; it's about fear and knowing that no one can protect a poor person from the power of drug kingpins. Hell, they've seen presidents assassinated and police chiefs snuffed. So they figure, what chance do they have—what chance does their entire network of family and friends have? Silence is golden. But I couldn't live with that sense of powerlessness."

"I'm really sorry to hear about your family," Davis said, after an awkward stretch of silence. Although his tone was professional, it contained an undercurrent of gentleness that she wished she hadn't heard.

"Thanks . . . but that was a long time ago. I'm all grown up now and survived. So you don't have to worry about me flipping out and blowing the man away in his sleep or anything crazy. Despite the circumstances, I am a trained professional."

"With a distinguished record, Hank Wilson informed me. Much respect, Special Agent Wagner." Davis nodded, keeping his eyes on the road. He paused as though trying to decide how to formulate the next question and then delivered it as though he were interviewing her for a Pentagon job. "When did you decide to go into law enforcement?"

"The day after I stopped crying and realized that nobody was going to testify or find the Salazars to lock them up." Sage kept her gaze on the passing highway landscape, not actually seeing it as her family's funeral flashed through her mind. "Figured if nobody from the outside could make a difference—at least, no one I'd ever seen in my old neighborhood had—then I'd get inside one day and fight them from the inside out."

"Like I said, much respect," he replied in a low, easy rumble. "But that decision has had to be hard on your grandmother and the rest of your family."

"My grandmother *was* the rest of my family," she said quietly. "My father died in a bottle long before my mother was murdered. But thank God I buried my grandmother before I went in deep."

She shook the memories and forced herself to return to the present. "So, do you have family who could be threatened, compromised, held hostage? If so, you may want to really decide how deep you want in or not—and there's no shame in that game. Screw that whole death before dishonor pledge, if you've got a five-year-old kid somewhere or a pretty wife that they'll hack up into pieces and ship to you. No disrespect, but it's different working stateside than being an armed combatant in a war overseas, Captain."

"First of all," he said in an easy, nonconfrontational manner. "Start practicing my alias—Juan."

"Right," she said, now looking at him. "Camille."

"Okay, Camille. Understand that I think that what you're doing is ten times riskier than what I've had to do in a unit."

She gave him a nod and kept her gaze on him

now. His comment went a long way in easing her ire about her professional territory being breached. "Thanks. Means a lot coming from a guy from DELTA Force."

"*De nada*. And for the record, I'm sorry that we met the way we did and that I accidentally trampled your setup. Won't happen again."

"I appreciate that," she said, losing the agitation from her voice.

"We really are on the same side, Camille. We both want the bad guys."

She nodded and kept her eyes on his profile, beginning to see past her anger and slowly beginning to notice how handsome he really was.

"Typically, we go in hard," he admitted, "do an extraction, blow a bridge, hit a target with dead-aim sniper fire, or track moving targets . . . but we don't live with the enemy. We do surveillance, but nothing as mentally and emotionally intense as what you're dealing with. We're in and out. Intelligence deals with going undercover."

"That's why I asked if you had people here you cared about," she said, leaning forward again and causing him to take another look over his shoulder. "I don't think I could handle being responsible for anything that might happen. Man . . . if you're half a world away in Iraq or Afghanistan, the chances of some highly intelligent nut-job finding your people is low. But if you've got family in Broward County or something, even a coupla states away . . ."

"I appreciate the concern, Camille, and hear you loud and clear. No. I'm solo, too." He seemed to sit up straighter in his seat, if that were somehow possible, and she watched him grip the steering wheel tighter. "Haven't had the lifestyle that would really allow for a wife and kids, yet. Been on the move. Lost my dad when I was two. He was a Marine—tour of duty in 'Nam. They told me he got out in 1970, but not before getting hit with Agent Orange. His health was always bad from then on, my mom said. He didn't last long past my second birthday. Died in seventy-nine. Had an older brother. The streets finally took him. Drug gang wars too."

"Must have been hard on you and your mom," she said quietly. "My grandmother always would say there was nothing worse than burying a child or her grandchildren."

"Yeah . . . My brother used to keep the neighborhood gangs off me. I looked up to him and he pushed me in school—said I was the one that would piece Mom's heart back together after he'd broken it. That's how I wound up in the military and, unfortunately, he wound up in a body bag on the streets of Chicago. But me being in the Service didn't glue my mother's heart back together—just made her scared to death that she'd lose me, too."

"Well, she can be proud of you . . . got to see you make it." Sage heard her voice soften as she said the words. The drug war in the streets at home had also struck Captain Davis in a profound way, making them fellow veterans of sorts. She hadn't wanted to know that, hadn't wanted to care about this new, forced partner.

"Cancer took my mother a few years back," he said in a quiet but matter-of-fact tone—the one that people use to disguise deep hurt. "But at least she didn't have to see me come home with a flag draped over my coffin. That's all she ever talked about not wanting to see. So I'm good."

"I'm real sorry to hear that," Sage murmured. She felt his statement at the pit of her stomach.

He simply nodded and allowed silence to linger between them for a while.

"No cousins and extended family?" She waited, understanding how saying it out loud and admitting that you were basically orphaned in the world was very different than just knowing it.

"I have some people in Arkansas . . . lotta folks I never got to know real well on my father's side. My mother's family was small and tight out of Chicago, but most of them are gone now. Nobody the enemy can make a direct link to." He lifted his chin and spread his massive hands around the steering wheel again as though resetting himself. "My unit is my family."

"Then we have that in common," she said,

fully appreciating where he was coming from. Her team members would be the only ones to attend her funeral, would be the only ones to lift a beer in her honor and maybe shed a tear or two when they ultimately lowered her casket into the ground.

Silence became a third passenger in the van as they exited the highway and entered South Beach's main thoroughfare. Yet, Captain Davis kept glancing up to his rearview mirror, his intense gaze seeming haunted.

"It's not my place to say this, but . . . are you sure this is a good idea, ma'am?"

"Camille, remember? Ma'am makes me sound old, by the way." She offered him a smile, sat forward, and placed a supportive hand on his shoulder as he turned into a covered parking garage.

The moment he navigated into a space, he turned around in his seat to fully face her. "Does your team have a GPS locator on you? Do you have enough artillery? If this guy gets pissed off—"

"I'm going to have to let him slap me around a bit for going off without his consent," she said as calmly as possible. "And, no . . . I've never allowed the government to put a chip in me. I'll be fine."

"Unacceptable. You already have a concussion and don't need to be reinjured."

"I know, Captain . . . but rest assured, as soon

as we get the word, I will kick his ass for the trouble."

She smiled, Captain Davis didn't.

"Juan, remember."

His surly reminder made her smile wider. "It's going to be all right, *Juan,*" she said.

"I don't want you to have to do anything in there that you don't want to." His statement was blunt and delivered with crisp military diction, but his intense dark gaze was definitely haunted. "You've given enough. We have all the intel we need. Whatever we don't know yet, we can gain through other methods. You shouldn't have to deal with that shit, no matter how badly we all want to bring these bastards down."

They sat in the dim parking lot staring at each other. It was a standoff where no one would mention the unmentionable, and yet this man whom she'd just met was trying his best to ask her to not go back in and put her body on the line.

Men had come and gone in both her personal and professional space; she'd had suitors, lovers, crushes, mentors, but had never truly allowed herself to become vested in the hopes and dreams of having anything that resembled a normal relationship. She could tell that this undercover scenario had to be unfathomable for a man like Captain Anthony Davis, someone who seemed to have a very straight-arrow, black-and-white view of the world. This was a man, she guessed, who had probably experienced normal relationships all his life. Her assignment undoubtedly contradicted everything he believed to be right with the world. She could only imagine that to him, she might as well have been an alien . . . and as she stared at his handsome face and deeply troubled eyes, for some reason now that made her very sad.

"I only have to be there for maybe another forty-eight to seventy-two hours. . . . That's when the delivery will probably go down, if they solidify the deal. My goal is to find out exactly when and where, then I'm out."

She slowly removed her sunglasses and captured Captain Davis's troubled gaze within her own. "I'll allow him to slap me around and then take off my makeup, so he'll think he's responsible for the bruises from the fight that you and I had. I'll weep and cower and make the man feel as badly as I can . . . and claim an inability to function. But with a stressful deal going down, his lack of time and patience, and my little tantrum for attention—which is how I'm sure he'll view my running away in a speedboat—I may be able to avoid being with him again. Understood?"

"And if not?"

Again, silence slipped into the spaces between them.

"I'll handle it."

Sage grabbed her large, gold-tone designer purse and slung it over her shoulder. She had no other answer for Captain Davis, beyond the one he didn't want to hear for some odd reason, and the one she didn't feel like saying out loud. His eyes seemed to beg for answers to questions she couldn't let herself think about right now.

There was pain and outrage in his gaze, but oddly no judgment as she placed her hand on the door and he popped the lock for her. He wore the expression of someone trapped within a reality he hated, unable to change what was, wishing with all his might that he could. The reality of her undercover assignment clearly violated everything the man before her believed in, yet for the sake of the mission, there was nothing either of them could do about it. The fact that he cared while not even knowing her was troubling on a level that was hard to sort out.

Sage lifted her chin and took in a deep, steadying breath. Captain Anthony Davis's gaze never wavered. She understood feeling powerless and knew that look in a person's eyes all too well. It was the same one that had once haunted hers. But until now, she'd never had a champion. Although he hadn't said that he was or wanted to be that for her, there was something unmistakable in the depth of the captain's angry eyes that let her know that he'd kill Salazar twice if he could.

She had to get away from that look before it crumbled her resolve. No man had ever seen through every layer and barrier she owned to peer directly at her soul and then ask it questions without uttering a word. And it had been so long since anything deep within her had stirred that the strange sensation of being secretly alive was unnerving.

Quickly opening the van door, she refused to theorize about the hundred things that could possibly go wrong. Captain Davis didn't need to know that; it would only add to his obvious worry. All he had to do was get the information he needed and then help her hunt the bastards they were after. That was all.

"Just don't die on me, Captain. You seem like a pretty decent guy, even if you did try to kill me."

Before he could respond, she was out of the vehicle and had slammed the van door behind her.

CHAPTER 4

He watched her walk away and not look back, the globes of her lovely rump a mesmerizing vision undulating beneath the tight white fabric. Her head held high and shoulders back, she strode forward like a Nubian queen. Each loud click of her gold stilettos against the concrete sent a stab into his nervous system. That jarring female-created sound then sent his gaze down the length of her long, shapely legs. His reaction was one born of pure male reflex, something he couldn't have stopped if his life had depended on it.

Everything professional within him said that he shouldn't have noticed these things about her. But everything male within him was on the verge of insubordination to his own direct order to stand down.

Sage Wagner was a problem. She wasn't just talented, capable, sexy, and smart—the woman had integrity. That was a rare quality these days. Plus, wrapped inside all that professional armor was a woman with an injured heart and a deeply wounded soul.

It would have been easier to deal with her if she was just some ice princess with a gun in her hand. She wasn't a person scratching and clawing her way to the top of a department for the sheer adrenaline rush that came from success . . . not that he would have cared one way or another if that was her personal bent. But hearing her story, knowing what she'd been through, and maybe more important, knowing how she'd survived it all by putting her entire being on the line, just messed with him. Profoundly so. From what little he knew about her, his gut told him that this woman was just as exquisite on the inside as she was on the outside; a quality rarer still.

And due to a communications glitch and overlapping missions, he'd not only hurt her physically, but he'd also put her in harm's way. Now he had to fix that, yet couldn't do a damned thing while some lowlife slapped her around at best, or severely beat and raped her at worst. To make matters absolutely more insane, she couldn't even protect herself once back inside Salazar's hostile camp, not without blowing her cover, all because of the marks he'd left on her.

If he'd only known . . . *damn*.

Anthony wiped his palms down his face and banged his forehead against the steering wheel as she disappeared into a brilliant swath of sunlight. From where he sat in the shadowy garage, it was like watching an angel simply vanish into the bright light. Wearing a smudged white dress and no visible means to protect herself, she was fearlessly walking back into a place where other angels feared to tread.

He had to fix this, had to make this right. The Salazars had to go down hard when he took down Assad. More than anything, however, he had to make sure that Special Agent Sage Wagner came home in one piece.

God help him make this right.

She had to get out of the parking lot, had to get to fresh air. Sage was practically jogging in her heels as she exited the garage and entered the main shopping boulevard.

For a moment the chemistry between her and Captain Davis had been thick enough to cut with a Bowie knife. It was an unexpected jolt to her system, something so off the wall and crazy that she knew it had to be a result of the concussion. Yeah, she'd definitely bumped her head.

She didn't do men on the job, didn't lose focus while working a case, and in this circumstance, any deviation from the plan was a great way to get

herself killed. Almost happened earlier, under-
scoring that point, so what the hell was her
problem?

Shaking off the attraction, she set her sights
on Avant Garde. Hopefully, Jeffrey wouldn't be
in, because if he was, there'd be an inescapable
discussion about her bruised arms and slightly
puffy cheek. She was more than a fav customer to
him; she was a friend. Therefore, he'd undoubtedly stand in front of her fitting room door with
his arms folded, giving her all the statistics about
domestic violence, and caring about her—and it
would break her heart to have to lie to him.

Sage hoisted her shimmering Louis Vuitton
shoulder bag up, feeling every body blow that
had landed, and squinted against the sun glare,
Dolce & Gabbana designer shades be damned.
But she had to play this out, finish what she'd
started, and she definitely couldn't afford to lose
focus for personal reasons at this juncture.

To even go there mentally was ludicrous. She
was living a totally fabricated life, built from
the ground up by careful planning and her agency's stealth. Birth records, phony high school records, false parental death certificates, bogus job
records, even a couple of traffic tickets thrown
in for good measure to go along with the fake
driver's license she carried in her purse beside
the credit cards in her false name. Everything
had been established to give her an entirely new

history so that when Salazar had her investigated, he'd come up with a vetted mate.

No man with Salazar's kind of assets and in his line of business was going to risk his empire on casual tail. The woman who got to get inside would have to be thoroughly background-checked after she'd piqued his interest and rebuffed him persistently . . . until he decided that she was potentially wife material, a trophy with the background of a Dominican nun. And that's what the DEA had given her, the background of a saint, down to the second-grade teacher's qualifications and Catholic school foundation.

Hesitating in front of the boutique, Sage stared at her reflection in the plate glass window. There was no room in this equation for how she felt or what she wanted. There was only the case, only the mission. She hadn't felt her body stir for a man in years. It had been ever longer since she'd been willing to tell someone what had happened to her family. Everything with Salazar was an act, an illusion just like her bogus ID. She hadn't ever choked up thinking back on it all because someone asked, "What did they do to you?" Captain Anthony Davis was a problem—one that she didn't have time for right now.

Sage pushed forward and swallowed hard, forcing the wet emotion that stung her eyes to burn away. Being tired didn't matter, and she didn't have time to bleed. After the mission was complete and the case file was closed, *then* she could think about what next.

She glanced around the small, airy space, glad that only the counter girl was there on her cell phone, and grabbed a few oversized white blouses off the rack. Her image from earlier in the day would be on the cameras at the mansion. A total wardrobe change was out. That might be a dead giveaway that something was awry. But a gauzy white blouse, put on over the tube dress and belted, could work. If asked, she could say she took it out of her purse when she got a little chilly from the water spray.

Sage held her long-sleeved choices against her body. Yeah, that could work. It would hide the smudges and her arm bruises, and if any dirt on the dress was seen she'd tell the truth—the boat was a bit dirty. Then she could complain about that, too. In fact, she could always say she fell into the boat, having tried to get in it with heels on, and then had to take her shoes off. Blah, blah, blah. A new plan was beginning to hatch in her sore brain.

Her mind was racing as she quickly made her purchase, put on the blouse right in the store, and hurried out of the boutique before Jeffrey returned. Without Avant Garde's inquiring owner slowing her down, she could quickly binge shop and then get to a table to call Bruno. From there, she'd just have to wing it.

* * *

Sage picked at her shrimp Caesar salad without really tasting it. But her glass of chardonnay had been refilled twice. Fatigue clawed at her body and her mind. She didn't immediately look up when Bruno's hulking form cast a shadow over her table.

"The boss has been looking for you," Bruno muttered in a deep rumble. "He's pissed."

"Yeah, I bet he is," Sage replied in a flat tone, not having to feign her indifference.

"Where've you been? We've been driving all over South Beach looking for you."

She glanced up at Bruno's massive frame, but strategically placed a palm against her left cheek while resting her elbow on the table. Her sarcastic expression said, duh—look at the bags in the chair, asshole.

After a moment he shifted his weight and folded his arms over his barrel chest, getting the message. She went back to slowly picking at her salad.

"Listen," he muttered with strain lacing his voice. "I know it mighta got a little crazy back at the house, but you can't be running off right now, okay? So, what the boss doesn't know doesn't have to hurt anybody . . . and there's no need to make a big deal out of anything."

Feeling the immediate advantage, Sage kept her eyes on her salad as she moved grilled shrimp around on her plate. So Bruno didn't want her to blow things out of proportion, huh.

"He's not going to be angry at *me,* you know that, right? Not for removing myself from earshot of you guys talking nasty. So, when I go back home and tell him that—"

"Look," Bruno said, now taking a seat across from her. "I know it got nuts back there, but he's not even home, all right. You don't have to get into the details of who said what . . . and I'm sorry if anybody offended you. The guys were just joking around . . . all of us were."

Sage kept a palm on her face covering the bruised left side of it, using her right hand to push lettuce leaves around in a circle with her fork. "He's not home yet?"

"No. He had to go to New Orleans, but he'll be back in a couple days, right after Mardi Gras— and you need to be back and tucked in safe with everything back to normal."

Now she looked up at Bruno, the gears in her mind turning quickly. This new information had to be communicated to her team and Captain Davis, stat. If the shipment was going down tonight, they needed to know that. Then again, it could have been a logistics dry run with Assad. Either way, it was valuable intel.

"He never told me he was going to New Orleans," Sage murmured, sounding dejected. "I might have wanted to go, too."

"Yeah, well, he didn't take any of us, so don't go making a big deal out of it. Maybe, if you behave yourself, after he's finished doing business, he might fly you down to join him, since it'll be Mardi Gras."

"Why couldn't he just take me right from the start?" she said, challenging Bruno with a pout. Inside, her heartbeat had kicked up a notch as panic set in, but she stayed calm on the surface so as not to tip him off.

Bruno leaned forward. "Look . . . I shouldn't be telling you anything, all right. Just know that he had serious business to take care of and wants you somewhere safe while he's away." Bruno sat back, looked around the restaurant, rubbed his jaw, and then lowered his voice to a plea. "C'mon, Camille. Gimme a break. Just come home."

"I'm not mad at you now; I'm more pissed at him. I would have loved to visit the Big Easy." She ate a few more bites of her salad, toying with the strain in the huge security guy who had been sent on a fool's errand to babysit her. She needed more answers. "He's probably got some hoochie in a room in New Orleans, that's why I couldn't go . . . probably cheating on me as we speak."

"No, no, and please don't go telling him I said anything about New Orleans, all right. It's not like that, it's strictly business."

"Really?" she murmured, looking up at Bruno with sad eyes.

"Really."

"Then, if it's not some other woman, why couldn't he take me this morning?" she whined.

"The man had to go check out his shipping warehouses, all right. That's all I can tell you. There's nothing fun going on down there, Camille. Honestly. You know he had a meeting at the airport with a big client . . . and I guess they wanted to see whatever—then he'll be back. So, are you coming home or what?"

She released a long sigh and stared at Bruno with the most innocent expression she could muster. "Can't you just tell him that you found me here and that I want to go to the spa to get a mani-pedi and massage and might even stay at the Ritz Carlton tonight . . . just so I don't have to rush home? I mean, what's to do at the mansion, especially if he's not there? Maybe I could even go have a drink with one of my girlfriends and go listen to some live music or go to a club, and get myself pretty for when he gets back."

Bruno briefly closed his eyes and smoothed a palm over his mousse-spiked blond hair. "He said to bring you home."

There was no way she was getting into any vehicle but the red Mercedes coupe that didn't have C4 wired under the chassis.

"Look, if you talk to him and tell him you found me . . . in fact, I'll even get on the phone while you call him, then he should be all right with that, right?"

"I dunno. He's got a lot going on right now. He's not in the frame of mind for trivial—"

"So now I'm trivial? Is that what he said about me?"

"No, no, no, no, no—you are taking things all wrong, Camille. The man wouldn't have sent a security detail over here looking for you if you were trivial. Think about it."

Power was in the eye of the beholder. She loved watching panic dance in Bruno's helpless eyes. The man had killed more people and broken more kneecaps than probably the DEA even knew about, and yet he was twisting in the wind over a recalcitrant woman who didn't want to get into his car. Priceless.

"Call him and let me talk to him, pleeeaaase?' Sage cooed. "I promise that I won't give him any grief about the dogs or what you guys were saying . . . and you can just have one of the drivers bring me my Mercedes so I can get around South Beach and can come home easy-breezy when I'm ready . . . You guys can also take the boat back from the marina. I mean, really, what's the big deal?"

She gave Bruno a look that told him, short of bodily carrying her out of there, which he knew full well that he couldn't do without causing a scene and thus a police issue, she would not be moved. He was also not stupid enough to put his hands on the boss's woman, so it was a standoff, pure and simple.

"All right!" he said, clearly peeved, and then whipped out his cell from his pants pocket. "But you'll owe me."

"Bruno . . . you're the best," she said with a sexy smile.

"Yeah, well, no telling if he'll go for it—and if he doesn't, don't shoot the messenger. I'm just doing my job." Bruno put the cell phone to his ear. "Found her, boss. She's just eating an early dinner over here and been shopping all day, judging from the bags."

She watched Bruno nod.

"Yeah, but see that's the thing . . . she wants to go to the spa to get a manicure and pedicure . . . a massage and stuff, and get all beautiful for you . . . then maybe she was gonna meet up with a coupla her girlfriends for a drink before coming back." He turned to the side and lowered his voice. "She's kinda giving me the blues about leaving right this second and wants to talk to you."

Bruno pivoted in his chair and held out the cell phone to her. "Here. He said to put you on."

"Baby . . ." she cooed, spinning in her seat so that Bruno could only see her right side, and not giving Roberto a chance to fire the first salvo.

"You will *not believe* my day! Thank God Bruno came over here and got me to not be so mad. Oh, the county is so inept and allowed mongrels to run over the property—and what happened after that, well, I just couldn't stand to pass by it, let alone watch it. So I left. I needed to be on the water to shake the sights and the sounds out of my mind. It was just so . . . so . . . oh, I cannot even describe it."

Still not allowing Roberto a chance to get a word in edgewise, she went on in theatrical feminine fashion. "Then I *fell*."

She paused for dramatic effect, which would give Roberto his first conversational entrée, and she hoped it would earn her a dose of sympathy. The plan worked. What was sure to be a stern directive from him mellowed when he asked how she had fallen.

"I was on the patio when one of the scraggly strays came up there and I almost fell trying to get away from it. I guess I was already off balance when I went running across the slippery grass in my heels and another one of those hounds scared me and I tripped. I bruised my arms, I bumped my cheek, and then I was so upset that I got into one of the small boats just to get away. Then I slipped again trying to get into the stupid boat and banged my shin," she added, allowing tears to rise and her voice to warble. "That's why I just want to go to the spa and unwind a little . . . maybe stay at the Ritz until you come home. And after all that upset, Bruno said you had business to take care of and weren't even coming home tonight—and *you didn't even tell me* when you left today."

She paused, listening to Roberto's vague explanation about how his meeting had morphed into an unexpected business trip, and was very careful not to reference New Orleans or to ask him any details. The more he thought she was ignorant of his whereabouts, the better, and the key was to get him on the defensive, on the explaining side of the verbal joust. That way, she could press for concessions—the main one she needed right now was space away from the compound to maneuver.

"But Bruno says I can't go to the spa or out to eat with my friends, or even stay at the Ritz until you come back. What's going on, Roberto? Is something wrong? And since when did Bruno become the boss of me? Why is everyone treating me like this today?"

Roberto's voice was firm and yet oddly consoling as he tried to make her think she was living in a fairy tale. "Baby, it's gonna be all right," he murmured, patronizing her. "Bruno is *definitely* not the boss of you, all right . . . don't cry. I just want you to be safe. Nothing's wrong, but the economy is bad and wealthy women are a target. So go easy on Bruno and do what he says security-wise . . . and I give you permission to go to the spa and go out with your girlfriends. If you don't want to go home and want to stay at the Ritz, just make sure Bruno knows where you are at all times. Put Bruno back on the telephone."

Triumphant, she turned back to Bruno, and now that her cover story had been accepted, she could allow him to see the puffy side of her face. Thanks filled Bruno's eyes for making him seem like he was her hero and was also following his boss's directive. Bruno gave her a brief nod when he accepted the cell phone from her.

"Yeah, boss. . . . Okay. I'll send Rico back here with her car. Yeah, yeah, two-man detail outside the spa, the Ritz, and any club she goes to. I'm on it."

Their eyes met as Bruno accepted his orders; she mouthed "Thank you." He nodded. As soon as the call ended, Bruno let out a long breath.

"You should put some ice on that," he said, studying her face, "before it turns into a real shiner."

CHAPTER 5

Getting rid of Bruno was fairly easy—she just handed the man all her shopping bags, kissed his cheek, and asked him to please take her loot over to the Ritz Carlton where she'd be checking in later. Oh, yes, and if he could be a sweetheart and get her a suite. There was nothing a security guy hated more than being made an errand boy for the boss's woman. But Bruno was in no position to argue. She'd just taken a lot of heat off his ass, so he owed her.

Quid pro quo allowed her to exploit her short-term hold over Bruno to give him something constructive to do, specifically, to get out of her face and let one of his other brutes watch her sashay down the street to the spa.

It wasn't that big of a deal, actually. Bruno only gave her a cursory scowl and complied. Everything was located along the open-air pedestrian mall on Lincoln Road. Thankfully, there was no need to get into one of the rigged vehicles with any of them—something she'd have to definitely talk to Captain Davis about at some point very soon.

Miami heat, speed bumps, and unwitting, innocent civilians were giving her the hives as she thought of the hundred and fifty things that could set off an accidental detonation.

But she had to get to the spa. The über upscale establishment was right next to her selected eating emporium, by design, just like the gym was right across the pedestrian thoroughfare. It was the only place she could make a safe call and visit regularly without suspicion. And just as membership had its privileges, so did being a regular spa-salon patron at the chic enterprise that was competing with all the services offered at the Ritz.

There, she had a permanent locker with a false back in it. Going to a salon and spa three times a week wouldn't raise suspicions. Roberto had been the one to insist that she quit her teaching job, move in with him, and become acquainted with a lavish lifestyle. She'd moved her contact cell, weapons, and backup ID from the hidden location within her school locker to the spa. Everything about the places she chose was strategic. She'd picked this particular spa, even above the Ritz Carlton's fabulous services, because given Roberto's jealousy and paranoia, if she made regular trips to a hotel, her virtue could be called into question. That would have been a dangerous complication. At a spa or at a non-hotel-related gym, her activities could be monitored easily by one of his goons.

To stay on the safe side, she even had a female personal trainer at the gym, one that she was almost sure Bruno was doing. However, the last thing she had to worry about was for one of Roberto's henchmen to follow her into the ladies' locker room at the spa, or barge in while she was getting a facial, or burst in to argue with the queen who was the undisputed czar of fashion in the hair salon section.

Sage entered the open, pristine sanctuary and felt her body relax. Light lavender and eucalyptus scents helped calm her wire-taut nerves. Soft, rippling wall fountains flowed in gentle currents over smooth stones.

"Hello, Ms. Rodriguez," a well-coiffed blonde intoned with a wide smile. Her smile faded a bit as worry entered her eyes. "Welcome . . . and what will we be able to help you with today?"

"Oh, thanks so much, Julie. I just have time for a mani-pedi, can you fit me in?"

"Of course we can," Julie mewed, opening the book. Then she looked up again, seeming as though she was trying to hold on to her professional distance, but not quite able to fully conceal her concern. "Chen Lee will be able to help you in a moment. We'll get you right back in a private room today, all right?"

"I just need to powder my nose," Sage replied. "Thank you so much."

"Of course. You know the way back to our lockers, right?"

"Definitely," Sage said with a smile. Julie's remark had been a mere courtesy; as a regular, they both knew that Sage knew the place inside and out. "Thanks again."

"You're more than welcome. There are fresh robes and slippers in the back, if you do decide to change your mind and get more done. You know we'll *always* accommodate one of our best clients . . . and all you have to do is tell whoever is giving you your services to adjust the pressure."

"Thanks," Sage said quietly and slipped away from the front desk toward the back of the spa.

Julie's discreet appraisal of her cheek said it all—we'll help move out the bruised blood and can treat this, but we know what happened and have seen this before.

A facial and massage were out of the question, even though it would have bought her time away from Bruno and his men. But the thought of anybody touching her face or body right now didn't seem appealing in the least, not when every inch of it ached.

Sage hurried to her permanent locker, glanced around quickly, and grabbed a metal file out of her purse. The moment she spun the combination and popped open her locker, she hung her purse inside the long, walnut enclosure. She peered around again; the other ladies were oblivious as she quietly removed the false metal back wall and felt for the contact cell phone that was duct-taped behind it. Then, as smooth as silk, she extracted it, dropped it in her bag, locked her locker again, and hurried to the bathroom closets.

Each stall was its own spacious mini chamber, complete with pedestal sink, floor-to-ceiling slatted walnut doors, a commode, and a fresh stack of hand towels and fragrant lotions and soaps. She waited, listening, and then dialed Hank Wilson, keeping the message brief as soon as he connected.

"You okay?" he asked quickly.

"Never better," she replied. "Target is in New Orleans—I've got a reprieve."

"Good." Hank released a long breath. "This means what?"

"Means he's either doing the deal as we speak or went there to do a drop-check at one of his warehouses. I can't confirm that, but my hunch is that he went to personally be sure the location is secure for his incoming inventory. I think he wants to make sure everything is airtight—locked and loaded—and he'd show that to his new, nervous supplier to reinforce that his word is his bond."

"We should be hearing something from Agent Alvarez in New York, soon, then—if your hunch proves correct, Wagner. Because as soon as Salazar gets his shipment, he's got to move it out and away from him as fast as possible."

"Right," Sage replied, and then cracked the stall door to peek out. "I'm gonna have to go soon, Hank, but Bruno said our target will be in Louisiana for a couple days, which leads me to believe that's when he'll divvy up the product for his distributors. But the shipment is definitely coming into New Orleans," Sage added in quick, low-toned bursts of information, listening between sentences for potential eavesdroppers. "He also didn't take his home security team. How much you wanna bet his A-team is positioned there? The real badass mercenaries. But he's nervous, has the B-team, Bruno and company, watching me and the house like he's ready for all hell to break loose from his original supplier."

"Man . . . I thought everything was gonna blow in Miami," Hank shot back.

"Me, too. But think about it. If his supplier needs arms, New Orleans is a good place to smuggle them out of with a base and naval air station down there. Flip some manifests, grease the right civilian palms, and it's not too difficult to make something seem like it's part of a military shipment from a government contractor.

"Plus, it's a port city and right there in the Gulf—with quick access to Mexico, which has practically nonexistent security on their docks, and from there to wherever in the world. Getting stuff from Mexico to Canada or whatever isn't a stretch. It's not like the Big Easy's infrastructure is fully back in place, and I don't have to tell you that their law enforcement is maxed out, hasn't come back since Katrina. Their port patrols are a whole lot softer than Miami's, by a long shot. So jump on it, Hank. Our target went to the airport this morning to meet his supplier and never came back. His jet may still be in the air if they had a long meeting first, for all I know . . . or they most likely did the meeting on the jet and could have landed hours ago. That's where the Captain's MI can help. You've got the call letters on the craft. Maybe satellite imaging will show him debarking, what vehicle they entered, and which warehouse they headed to, et cetera."

"We're on it," Hank said, quickly. "What else do you need, Wagner?"

"Tell my new best friends, Jacqueline and Suzanne, to listen for a cell phone call from me early this evening—like eight or nine P.M. I'm supposed to be hanging out with my girlfriends and having a drink."

"Done. I'll let agents McCoy and Whittaker know." Hank paused. "You be careful."

"Hank, I'm good. I'm about to get my nails done."

She hung up and closed her eyes, fighting fatigue, and then something within made her fingers dial the number that she'd memorized during the van ride over to South Beach.

Captain Davis picked up on the first ring. She hesitated a moment and she could tell he was waiting to ID her voice.

"Captain?"

"Roger. What's your status?"

"I'm all right."

This time he hesitated, and it gave her a chance to process the deep baritone concern that resonated in his voice. The sound bottomed out in the pit of her stomach until her entire midsection clenched.

"Copy that," he said. "Your location? Are you safe?"

"At the spa. Yes. And there was a development. Hank will fill you in. Your target is currently in New Orleans. I'll be at the Ritz Carlton on Lincoln tonight, and maybe tomorrow as well. But I'm being watched."

Again, there was a hesitation and she could hear silence crackle on the line.

"Were you injured before the target left Miami?"

"No," she said quietly. "I never had to deal with that, and it looks like I'll have a few days to heal. Security will be watching me while he's out of town, so I cannot deploy to New Orleans—again, Hank will fill you in. Do you understand?"

"Affirmative. I'll be in touch, one way or another. Copy?"

"I copy," she said, holding the telephone more tightly. "But I have to go."

She disconnected the call when she heard her manicurist calling for her.

"Ms. Rodriguez? I'm ready for you whenever you are ready. I just wanted to let you know . . . but please take your time."

"Coming in a moment," Sage called out in a forced, upbeat tone and then flushed the toilet. She let the water run a bit in the sink and washed her hands, slathering on soap, then lotion for complete authenticity. Reversing her earlier actions, she returned the encrypted cell phone to her locker and then went to meet Chen Lee.

The moment the young woman appraised her cheek with sad, worried eyes, Sage sighed.

"You know what . . . can you ask Julie if they have some kind of organic facial and maybe light massage treatments that can heal bruises? Or maybe just an ice pack?"

"We do," Chen Lee said in a graciously quiet

murmur. "That, plus soothing treatments, and the hot and cold pools, along with other water treatments will help."

The call to Sage Wagner ended, but the impact of hearing her voice and knowing that at the moment she was all right, lingered. The urge to go to her, to see with his own eyes that she was really okay, was an irrational impulse that he had to wrestle. The muscles in his biceps twitched with the need to move, to thrust himself into action, as he pushed the remains of his lunch away and looked around the small restaurant.

There was no justifiable reason he'd stayed in South Beach, other than the fact that he'd wanted to be nearby . . . just in case he got an SOS call from Sage—which was ridiculous, now that he'd actually heard from her.

Despite all the beautiful people parading around South Beach, that wasn't why he'd stayed. He could give a damn about bikini-clad coeds or vacuous celebs spending crazy amounts of money in chichi shops and eateries when he had a mission to focus on.

He'd stayed to check on Sage. That was the undeniable truth. But that, in and of itself, was insane and off mission. He wasn't her body guard. She was a trained agent, able to take care of herself. He had to get his head together.

Rather than dwell on the two and a half hours

he'd wasted riding around the area, supposedly familiarizing himself with the terrain—which, if he was honest, really amounted to little more than stalling for time and eating lunch while he hoped to figure out the impossible—he called Hank Wilson like Sage instructed. He got Hank on the second ring. The intel that Sage had been able to gather in a couple of hours blew Anthony's mind.

Her intel from the ground, and from her position inside, was so much more effective than what he was getting at a distant, ten-thousand-foot aerial view. Although a lot of it was still laced with speculation, he trusted her gut hunches. They were logical possibilities coming from one tough, savvy, sexy woman on the inside.

He listened to Hank relay the update and could corroborate a lot of it from his side as well. According to MI, the targets weren't making a lot of the usual mistakes, like sloppy cell phone chatter, e-mails, and other common leaks. It took one well-positioned agent on the inside to get what they needed. Therefore, to his way of viewing the world, Sage Wagner had to live long enough to be decorated for that kind of heroism.

"Agent Alvarez informs us that the top five distributors in Salazar's camp will be coming together to take the product right before Mardi Gras—and it appears that the Salazars are also assisting Assad with brokering some weapons holding locations up in Canada through his northeast network. Salazar is in this waist-deep with Assad. So our agent is going to have to introduce you in Miami within the next day or so to get you inside," Hank said. "Are you ready?"

"Affirmative," Anthony stated flatly. "My chain of command is already aware of the unusual circumstances and I have clearance to proceed."

"Good," Hank replied. "Nice to have the army on our side going after this bullshit."

As soon as Anthony disconnected the call with Hank Wilson, he phoned his team, driving hard toward the airport.

"I need a bird out of Miami International and I need an eleven-man unit on the ground in New Orleans. Copy?"

"I copy, Captain," Lieutenant Hayes said. "Will get a bird cleared and a drop team ready to rock and roll. Will also position a tractor trailer in both locations with portable choppers from the 160th Airborne."

"Roger that. Also put our MI eye in the sky on a private Gulfstream III, ID—Alpha, Charlie, Tango, three, five, niner—copy?"

"I copy. Will send sat images to your encrypted cell phone and laptop. Should be able to give you a time of landing, debark, and will do our best to track where their vehicles are headed, sir."

"Their destination has got to be somewhere

near the docks. Our partner agency's target has warehouses there and I've been informed that's where the party went. There's a high probability that's how they're gonna bring the product in— by shipping containers. But position our unit at NAS and the Joint Reserve base to be ready for a boots-on-the-ground assault backed up by a couple of Apaches."

"Your contact at DEA confirmed New Orleans as a new target site?"

"Affirmative. High probability that contraband coming in will be done on false shipping manifests. Weapons going out in that large a quantity are going to have to pass through shipping manifests, too. Could be headed toward Mexico en route to Canada—it just can't happen on the ground by truck, if it's coming from a US source. Trucks are too easy to search and seize. Large vessels are a search nightmare and are practically safe once in international waters where maritime law applies. But cash can be as simple as a wire transfer or as old school as loaded in car trunks."

"Any word on a weapons source yet, Captain?"

"Negative. Inform chain of command that our blind spot is the fact that we do not have a lock on the weapons buy yet, which can happen in Europe or anywhere in the world from old Soviet stockpiles. We have a lead link to Canada—and DEA is positioning my entry into that scenario as we speak. Remember our mission is to not only apprehend our primary target and disrupt the deal, but to also find out the source of his weapons buy and to seize his cash. Relay our updated intel to the commander via chain of command, Lieutenant."

"Roger, Captain. Rendezvous in New Orleans. Hooooah!"

CHAPTER 6

Sage slid onto the bar stool at the Ritz Carlton and exchanged air kisses with Special Agents Andrea McCoy and Cheryl Whittaker, aka Jacqueline Perez and Suzanne White. Strategically positioning herself so that her back was to the men guarding her while facing her friends, Sage ordered a club soda and lime. The setup allowed the two female agents to keep an eye on Bruno and his men while she appeared detached.

Soft music was playing at the piano bar, which was a wondrous relief to the mild headache that still intermittently nagged her. Doing a nightclub at this point was completely out of the question. The throbbing music and tight crowds within a South Beach hot spot would have been like driving a railroad spike through her temple. The less chaos the better.

To Bruno and his small security team, who were enjoying beers and Jack Daniel's at the far side of the room, it appeared that she was just joining up with her old college and teacher girl-friends. Perfect.

Pretending not to notice the bar's extra set of bouncers, Sage focused on the agents who were her cover for passing information and receiving information. Although a nap had helped, and the spa treatments had gone a long way in soothing her body aches and removing some of the bruis-ing, what she wanted most was eight to ten solid hours of sleep. But that was not to be had.

"How're you feeling?" The agent posing as Jacqueline pushed a long spill of auburn hair behind her ear and took a sip of her Dewar's on the rocks.

"I'll live," Sage said, smiling, and giving Jac-queline the eye to stay in character.

"Love the outfit," the agent playing the role of Suzanne said.

"Thanks," Sage replied, gesturing to the royal blue, plunging neckline, Victoria's Secret blouse and Angel bra she wore with long costume jew-elry chains over tight black jeans and a pair of spike Manolo Blahnik heels. "Jeffrey is going to be so mad that I didn't get this from Avante Garde. But I'll make it up to him soon." She took a sip from her drink when it arrived. "Are they still looking?"

"No. We're good. Your Vanna White fashion routine convinced them there's nothing to see, people, just three airhead chicks talking crap about nothing." Suzanne patted the edges of her frosted blond hair as she lifted her glass of merlot with a wry smile. "I say we have a ladies' night toast to seal the impression. Shall we?"

The three women lifted their glasses and brought them together with a light clinking sound. From the corner of her eye Sage could see Bruno and his men watching the football game on the soundless bar TV and desperately trying to get whatever bits and pieces of the game they could on their smart phones.

"I think we're good to go," Sage announced. "The ladies' night toast was a lovely touch."

The three agents laughed.

"So talk to me." Sage glanced from one agent to the next. "And tell me with a smile, Jackie."

Jacqueline pasted on a smile and lowered her voice. "Agent Alvarez up in New York confirmed what you'd heard from the big blond this afternoon. Your man is going to be doing the distribution deal down in New Orleans, right before Mardi Gras, so he can maneuver and play off of the chaos and the float trucks coming in and out, but not before he brings his inner circle together there. He's got to be sure there are no leaks before he tries to move that much weight, otherwise Guzman will be calling for his dick on a silver platter in Colombia."

Suzanne nodded, and spoke through a strained

smile. "Our New York team is going to get that DELTA Force captain into that meeting. DELTA wants to know about the weapons end of the deal; it looks like your man has a hand in that as well."

Leave it to Salazar to try to get paid on both sides of the transaction. Sage threw her head back and released a hearty feminine chuckle for theatrical effect to keep Bruno's men none the wiser about their conversation. "Really? Now that's just rich."

"Isn't it though?" Suzanne agreed, glancing at Jacqueline.

"He's gonna make a profit off the low-cost product, flip it at normal prices, and then will probably get some type of brokerage fee for making the weapons dealer connection." Sage just shook her head.

"Ex-Soviet dudes out of Canada, same ones who—get this—also on the third pass off from wholesaler, to distributor, to street retailers, help move your man's weight up and out through part of his upstate New York network," Jacqueline added, glancing at Suzanne. "That's why DELTA and Central Intelligence, along with the Feds, are all over this now. It's international, with links to terrorist cells up in Canada, and is considered a border threat. Captain Davis is the tip of the spear, and he's convinced his chain of command to let him be the one to get inside—

even though CIA usually handles such a role. But I guess the quick turnaround nature of things led to that. Not sure why the dude lobbied so hard for the role."

"Maybe because he tried to break my jaw and gave me a concussion?" Sage said with a wink, chuckling for Bruno's crew, but very sobered by what she was hearing.

"This thing is way bigger than we knew, Sage," Suzanne said. "It was always dangerous— but now it's ridiculous. Illegal drugs and terrorism have tangled tentacles all over the world. So you watch your back in there."

Sage nodded and sipped her drink, her mind reflexively returning to Captain Davis. "When's Alvarez going to position the new man in from DELTA?"

"Don't know yet. They're all down in New Orleans as we speak, trying to get a confirmation that the shipment came in and to get a bead on the containers and warehouse locations," Jacqueline replied.

Sage glanced at Jacqueline's Dewar's. "I should have ordered one of those. Let's just hope our DELTA Force captain doesn't get all gung ho and screw this up."

A list of all of Salazar's regional holdings scrolled on Captain Davis's encrypted data screen from the DEA field report. He held the smart device

next to Lieutenant Hayes so he could read off
the company and subsidiary names while corre-
lating that to all area warehouses listed in the MI
database. With a cut-and-paste feed, they waited
until two large structures finally lit as a match,
and then they relayed that back to the other
members of the unit that was waiting at NAS
for orders to move out.

Half the team would stake out the warehouse
area in readiness for any contraband movement,
the other half would use the intel that came in
from Central Intelligence to locate the shipping
containers with the drugs. Once that was done,
they would hold their position, ID how the drugs
would be disguised and transported, and follow
the product from the docks to the warehouses.

His men were to monitor the situation from the
ground, make sure no product moved from the
warehouses, and to follow Assad and the money.
His objective was to get inside, find out when the
money-for-weapons handoff would occur, and
to then drop the hammer on Assad and the arms
dealer, busting up that terror cell.

Lieutenant Hayes shut off his encrypted device and stashed it inside his fatigue leg pocket.
Captain Davis did the same. Both soldiers nodded as their eyes met and then dropped down
their night-vision goggles.

The docks were eerily quiet and they moved
along the shadows with practiced stealth. Within

fifteen minutes, they'd identified the Uzbekistani freighter. But gaining access to the ship, checking each of the huge containers, and carefully opening whatever disguising apparatus was being used—and then putting it back in place—could easily take all night.

Davis rubbed the nape of his neck, deciding where to begin. Through logical deduction, they could possibly narrow down the options by looking at the shipping manifest that had been transmitted to them earlier. It would be like searching for a needle in a haystack, trying to find any incoming product shipments that would relate to the types of legitimate products Salazar moved. Institutional canned foods, fabrics for prison uniforms, construction materials, anything related in any way to Salazar's legitimate operations would be the place to look first.

Uzbekistan was an exporter of building supplies, cement, marble, furniture glue, cellulose, and even saltpeter, not to mention its rich oil deposits and minerals. But oil and precious minerals weren't on the ship's manifest. Salazar had several construction firms. Looking for heroin and cocaine bricks inside bags of cement seemed like the most logical place to start.

Using hand signals, shedding their rucksacks and concealing them, they split up to silently throw secure lines from the dock to the ship for an arduous hand-over-hand stealth boarding. The moment they were on deck, they cut their lines and secreted themselves away, hugging the shadows, hunting for the numbered containers that held thousands of pounds of bag cement.

Onboard security was lax and avoidable. But opening the locked containers would take a little time. Locks would have to be cut and replaced if the ship master keys Intelligence provided didn't work. Hayes gave him a nod as they approached the back of a container they'd been seeking. Davis tapped his chest twice. He had the container keys provided by a Central Intelligence handoff. But footsteps and the sound of metal scraping made him hold up his fist.

They glanced at each other. Someone was already inside a container three rows over. There were six long aisles of containers filled with cement mix bags alone, and it was looking like fate had saved them a little trouble that night.

"Hurry up and take the pictures," a low, hissing voice urged. "Then be sure to put it back together and hide it in the stack. C'mon!"

"Shut up! I'm going as fast as I can!" another voice hissed. "But do you want to come back with blurry photos and have to answer to Guzman for that?"

Davis and Hayes hugged the steel frame of the container as they listened to the rapid fire of a camera shutter. After ten minutes, only the shuffle of footsteps could be heard as the container door banged shut and the lock clicked. They waited a full ten minutes, checked to see if the coast was clear, and then quickly opened and entered the container.

Hayes nodded and shined a light on the cement while Davis went to the back and began loading out stacked bags until he found one that had been punctured with a knife. Unsheathing his Bowie, he allowed his blade to follow along the same path that had been cut in the sack, careful not to spill cement, and then stuck it into the brick. Tasting the edge of his knife with the very tip of his tongue, he nodded and then hastily repositioned the compromised bag into the center of the heap.

Listening again, they waited a beat, and then quickly exited the container and locked it. Running in bursts, they stopped at every opening where moonlight could reveal them, hugged a container, and then dashed into another shadow until they reached the massive deck rails.

But debarking was going to be more hazardous than their entry. The two men who worked for Guzman were obviously still on board and skulking around as part of the security crew. Yet it was clear they all had the same objective—no one wanted to alert Salazar that they knew he was trying to double-cross Guzman. This added complication, that Guzman was very aware he was being double-crossed, was a dangerous wrinkle in the plan, one that MI, Central Intelligence, and DEA needed to know about stat.

Motioning for his lieutenant to go first so he could cover him, Davis watched Hayes make it to the dock shadows and disappear before he dropped a line and froze. Voices and approaching footsteps made it impossible to cast the line to the dock. Instead he had to bail over the edge straight down in a quick but silent descent into the murky water. Then came the waiting while the men had a cigarette and finally left to make their rounds again. As soon as the coast was clear, Hayes silently dropped him a line from the dock.

Once in the shadows with rucksacks back in place, they used Hayes's waterproof equipment to upload information about the container numbers and to communicate what they'd learned to their chain of command. The next call he made was to Hank Wilson, once Sage's encrypted cell rolled over to voice mail.

"If Guzman has spies and knows about Salazar's deal with Assad, but hasn't acted yet, then he's probably waiting until Salazar pulls in all his closest men to find out who his inner circle is before he smokes them. You've gotta get your agent out of there. She's a sitting duck as long as she's perceived to be Salazar's woman."

Davis gripped the encrypted cell phone and stared at Hayes as he spoke to Hank. The dank, oily water had soaked through his fatigues, but it was hard to tell which chilled him more—that or his worry about Sage Wagner.

"Both of my decoy agents are already gone for the night," Hank said, sounding frantic. "She doesn't have access to her encrypted cell phone and there's no way to get word to her tonight without compromising her cover in Miami. They'll go for Salazar first while he's in New Orleans, then—"

"What room is she in at the Ritz?"

He ignored the glance of concern Hayes shot in his direction.

"Twelve fifty-five," Hank said cautiously.

"Have an agent call her from the desk citing a plumbing problem. Get her to move to a room that Salazar's security goons didn't arrange for her, so that she knows she can speak freely. If they're in an adjoining suite now or something, that'll bust up the party." Davis looked at his watch. "I can be there in two hours."

CHAPTER 7

The sound of her hotel room phone ringing gave her a start. Sage looked at the unit and quickly picked it up. She hadn't been in her room a good five minutes, not long enough to take her shoes off and get settled, and now Bruno was calling?

But it wasn't him or one of the security guys. She recognized Dan's voice instantly. Her stomach clenched as she braced for the worst. Dan wouldn't have made contact like this unless the matter was urgent.

His message was terse. "Hello, ma'am. This is hotel maintenance. There's a leak in the stack pipe of your toilet that is unfortunately impacting the room below yours. We hate to inconvenience you, but need to move you to another suite. Will that be all right?"

"Yes . . . yes, of course," Sage replied in a wary tone. As soon as the call disconnected, she quickly grabbed her weapon, checked the magazine on it, hid it in her purse, then gathered her shopping bags and the small toiletries kit she'd gotten at the spa.

Dan arrived at her door wearing a hotel maintenance uniform. His blue eyes held a level of panic she couldn't decipher. But before he could give her a message, Bruno's door swung open with a slam.

He stood in his doorway for a moment wearing only a pair of black jeans and no shirt, frowning. "What's going on?"

Sage gave Dan a warning with her eyes to be cool and not to move. It was like doing a standoff with a Doberman. As long as it snarled and didn't advance, the more still you remained, the better your chances.

"Drama," she said with an airy wave of her hand. "Seems the seal or whatever in my toilet stack busted in the wall or whatever, and it's leaking down to the floor below. So they've gotta move me." She sucked her teeth and shrugged. "They slap all these buildings up in a blink of an eye these days, what can ya do?"

"Where're you moving her? I've gotta go check out the room." Clearly annoyed, Bruno kept one hand behind him, concealing his gun, while he body-blocked Sage from peeking into his room. No doubt he had company since the boss was away and guarding her was fairly light detail.

"Oh, don't be silly," Sage said, heading to the

elevator with Dan. "It's just a little leak. I'll call you from whatever room they put me in."

Bruno hesitated, and that's when she knew she had him. "You sure?"

"Yeah. It's been a long day. All I want to do is lie down."

Again Bruno hesitated. "Well, hit my cell as soon as you get settled, all right? I want me and the guys to be able to do hallway patrols and to know where you are."

Sage let out a long sigh and offered him a bright smile. "Bruno . . . this isn't the compound. It's *the Ritz*. Hallway patrols? Really? I promise to tell Roberto you guys walked the nap out of the carpet pacing back and forth in front of my room until I screamed at you to let me go to sleep. Deal?"

Bruno smiled, even though he was still frowning. "You call me and give me your room number as soon as you get settled."

"Okay, already," she said, laughing and then led Dan down the hall toward the elevators. She didn't look at Dan, but kept her eyes fastened to the elevator doors and spoke loud enough for Bruno to hear her. "So I take it I have to go down to the desk, get a new key, blah, blah, blah?"

"Yes, ma'am," Dan said nervously as they got onto the elevator. "Again, we apologize for the inconvenience."

The moment the elevator doors closed behind them, Dan began to fill her in with rapid bursts of information.

"Guzman knows? Shit! That is such not good news," she said quickly, looking at the descending lights.

"You're telling me?" Dan looked at the numbers for a second and then focused on her. "The room next to your suite is vacant. Leave the lock off. Hank wants you covered, if Colombians are about to go to war, and he's putting someone capable in there to watch your six. When you get to the lobby, you're registered in room 712, but your key works in room 217. Give Bruno 712. I'll put the television on in there. This way, anybody that could be looking for you in the hotel or following Bruno on rounds, whatever, will get an empty room. Got it? And if he somehow goes there and gets wise, the girl at the front desk is one of ours, and will pretend to have made a dyslexic type of mistake, all right? Just don't shoot first and ask questions later, if the adjoining room door opens. That's one of ours, Hank said."

Sage nodded as the elevator stopped at the lobby floor. "You go on and get out of here, Dan."

He pressed a key into her hand and held it briefly. "I'll be glad when this is all over and we all can stop worrying about you."

She brushed his cheek with a platonic kiss

just before the doors opened. "Get out of here, kiddo. That's a direct order. Everything is gonna be fine."

A quick shower at the base, a change into civilian clothes, a chopper flight into South Beach, a soft landing on top of an office complex heliport, and he was out. The unmarked vehicle was waiting for him in the underground parking lot beneath the building, unlocked. Keys were beneath the visor, along with a hotel room key.

He dropped his black weapons bag on the seat beside him. That, right now, was the only luggage he needed.

Sage sat in the dark, facing the adjoining door in her room with a gun in her hand. She'd called Bruno from her cell phone, not the room phone, and he hadn't sounded worried. A couple of agents were walking the halls dressed as hotel security to be sure Bruno didn't decide to check it out on the seventh floor after all. No calls meant good news.

And although Hank might have sent one of their agents in, she was too aware that a lot could happen between now and the time that person arrived to take the room next to her suite. What if the other side was aware of the switch? What if one of Guzman's mercenaries forced his way in with the new agent just to get to her? There was no telling until a visual ID was made.

When she heard the outer door of the next room quietly open and close, she stood up and steadied her weapon. A light tap at the door just caused her to tighten her grip. The door slowly opened and it took a moment for visual recognition to kick in. Adrenaline made her trigger finger tremble.

"Isn't this how we met?"

She lowered her weapon and let out an inaudible breath. Captain Anthony Davis's voice thrummed through her belly. "Yeah, but how about a cup of Joe instead of a concussion this time?"

He didn't respond, just lowered his gaze. She'd meant to make him smile.

Sage dragged her fingers through her hair and set her weapon down on the coffee table. "Bad joke," she said in a quiet voice, and then hugged herself. "I've never had anybody voluntarily come back for me. Guess I don't know what to do with that."

He discarded his weapon on the television cabinet, turned slowly, closed the door between their rooms, and spoke to her without looking at her. "I've never hit a woman in my life . . . much less put one in danger because of something I did. I just wanted to personally make that right."

"It wasn't your fault . . . and Hank would have sent over another agent to babysit me. You've got more important things to do, and I can take care of myself."

Captain Davis didn't move, didn't say a word, and again she knew she'd put a hard cement wall between them—one that wasn't necessary at this juncture.

"Hey, look . . . I'm sorry," she said, hugging herself tighter. "Apology accepted. And, remember, I had a nine pointed at your skull. I would have kicked my ass too, if it meant that I'd live. And all I was saying was, that you didn't personally have to come back . . . the agency—"

"Might have made a mistake and relayed the information to you too late." His voice was a low rumble of truth as he stared at her in the dark. Moonlight spilled on only his shoes, leaving him cloaked by the shadows. "I almost killed you because of bad intel, late intel. If there was a communication glitch and you weren't informed and something happened, it would . . ." His voice trailed off and he drew in a deep breath. "I couldn't reach you any other way."

She swallowed hard and nodded. "Thank you." After a moment of staring at his intense gaze in the dark, she glanced away. "How about that coffee, Captain?"

"I'd appreciate it, but not Captain between us."

"Right . . . Juan," she said, remembering his alias.

"No. As Anthony."

Again she just stared at him for a moment. Yes, Anthony . . . the man who'd returned to personally ensure her safety . . . a man who'd just asked her to drop his rank and alias to let her know that this unspoken thing went beyond a mere job or even duty. He was standing there clearly ready to take a bullet for her, and not necessarily in the name of God and country or the current mission.

"All right, Anthony," she murmured, and moved through the dark to get the coffeepot. "Cream and sugar?"

"Just sugar, not a lot."

He hadn't moved from where he stood by the door, shoulders back, head held high, senses on what seemed to be full alert.

She motioned toward the chair that was by the sofa. "Why don't you have a seat? It'll only be a few minutes."

He complied without argument, bringing his weapon near to set on the coffee table. "Did you get a full report?"

"Dan only gave me the highlights. But why don't you give me the details while this brews."

She listened intently as Captain Davis filled the empty spaces inside her with his low rumbling voice. The vibration of it and the caring within

it warmed her to her very core, and then radiated heat throughout her limbs. In all the years
she'd spent alone with just her and her Nana, all
she'd known at the hands of men was competi-
tion, abuse, heartache, and lies. No one had ever
come back to check on her to see if she was truly
all right.

Handing Davis a cup, she took a seat on the
small ottoman across from him in the dark and
stared at him.

"Thank you," she murmured and then took a
sip of too-hot coffee. "You even had a small unit
disarm the cars you'd set to blow?"

He nodded. "When I drove around South
Beach this afternoon and saw that the security
vehicles were tailing you through heavily com-
mercial areas with civilians, that was one of the
first calls I made. Two good men in my unit got
to them when you were in the piano bar. It was
the first opportunity we had, given the target's
security forces were with the vehicles until then."

Sage briefly closed her eyes. "When I think of
what could have happened . . ."

"Exactly my concern, too," he replied, now
sipping his coffee but never breaking eye contact
with her. "Those guys were giving their rides
to valets and double-parking outside of retail
stores . . . that wasn't in the plan. Collateral damage of that magnitude is not acceptable on my
watch. We thought we were going in to blow the

compound and cripple unmanned vehicles in the private garage. Things changed."

"Things always change," she said. "That's the nature of the beast."

"And that's exactly why I'm here."

They looked at each other for a long time, and finally she shook her head.

"You're here for more than a mission change or a complication," she said just above a murmur. "That's what worries me."

When he looked away, she placed a light hand on his knee. "I'm a really screwed-up person, Anthony. I'm not a solid bet. But I'm an ace in a firefight. That's all I really know how to do. And after this case closes, if I live, I don't have a clue what I want to do next . . . it damned sure isn't this anymore. Going in this deep once was enough. But this is all I'm cut out to do. Sad truth is, I've spent so long wanting to bring down the Salazar drug empire and invested so heavily in hating them that, once that happens, then what? I don't even know how to be a regular civilian with a normal life."

"Then we're not that different. I have no idea how to do anything but this. Once we break up this cell, another will grow in its place. I've been at this for years, busting terror cells . . . and there's no end to the cancer. Makes the soul weary after a while."

She withdrew her hand from his knee and hugged herself with one arm, clutching her coffee cup. "Can I be honest with you? I mean, really speak off the record here?"

He nodded. "Sage, we are so off the record that a record doesn't exist right now."

"Yeah . . . true." She took another sip of coffee, trying to find a way to allow the words to flow past her lips. "I don't want to do this job anymore," she said slowly closing her eyes. "But I'm in too deep and there's no way out other than to finish it."

She opened her eyes, surprised to find her vision blurry from unshed tears. Her voice quavered from emotion that she refused to allow to spill out with the truth she'd just told. Why did this man affect her like this? Extreme fatigue was the only reasonable answer. That, or something too dangerous to think about.

"Just like anyone else, I want a normal life," she admitted in a low murmur when he didn't jump in to offer any rebuttal. "I want all the horrible memories of what happened to me and what I've done, gone . . . but God help me, I don't know how to make that happen."

"Neither do I, Sage," he said in a mercifully quiet tone. "I don't know how to forget all the missions, all the deaths, and everything I wished I'd told the right people at the right time."

Sage swallowed hard again and set her coffee down on the floor by her feet. There was an unspoken confession hidden behind Anthony Davis's words, and just knowing that made her heart ache for him. "Tell me what happened?"

"Not much to tell, other than I could have come back for my brother . . . could have maybe saved his life, if I'd told the right people when and where they were going to rumble. I didn't. He and his gang were outgunned and outmanned three to one—but he'd told me not to come back there. Made me promise to keep everything on the low. He said he'd be all right. Until that night, he always was, and I didn't want to be responsible for snitching to possibly land him in prison. But I had knowledge that could have gone to the authorities . . . but . . ."

"But you were *a kid,*" she said firmly. "I grew up in the hood, too. There was a code. You and I both overcame that early conditioning later."

"Later was too late, and that code got my brother dead."

"But *you* didn't get him dead." She took up Anthony's free hand and squeezed it, all too familiar with the pain he tried to conceal. "Listen to me—you know that if he and his gang were hell-bent on rumbling another gang, it would have only been a matter of time before they settled that beef by having a showdown somewhere else. Bullets were going to fly, some kid in that

mix was going to get shot, along with any un-
lucky passersby. If the cops went in there blazing, your brother still stood a fifty-fifty chance
of getting shot and/or going to prison for a very
long time."

Anthony took a deep swig of his coffee and
set it down on the coffee table beside him. "True,
but I swore to myself from that point forward
that I'd always come back for my own . . . would
personally make sure that if I knew anything
that could keep someone alive, I'd get it to the
right place fast."

"And I promised that I'd be a part of the solution, and not a part of the problem after everything happened to my family," she said softly. "I
was too afraid, back then, to tell the police what
people in the neighborhood were saying . . .
knowing that no one would back me up or protect me."

"I've got your back on this one, Sage."

"I know," she murmured. "That's what scares
me."

She could tell from the troubled look in his
eyes, even sitting in the dark, that he thought she
was afraid of him. That wasn't it at all.

"I know I hit you, and vets sometime have
a bad rep . . . but . . ."

She placed a finger against his lips. "Don't. I'm
not afraid of you attacking me, having a flash-
back, or anything like that. I know you're not

some dude with a jacked-up psychological profile." She stared at him and then drew back from him and wrapped her arms around her waist. "I don't know what's happening here between us or why. All I know is that I have a role to play and from the moment I met you, for some really bizarre reason, I can't go back in and fake being with some man that I despise—and *that's* dangerous. That's what scares me."

"I don't know what's happening either, Sage, but I want to find out. Technically, I'm not even supposed to be here," he said quietly. "this is so off-mission that if I had to stand in front of a military tribunal to explain my actions, I couldn't. My only defense would be, I took one look at you and couldn't leave you in there with those animals. I know what can happen to a hostage. I can't let you become one."

"Don't do this, Captain," she whispered and then hugged herself tighter. "I haven't allowed myself to go deep into anything real in a very long time, and what I'm feeling right now is way more terrifying than facing Salazar."

"The fact that I'm sitting here without a plausible explanation for being here scares me, too. The mission is front of mind, don't get me wrong. I know what we've both gotta do. But you're also right up there sharing that same space and I've never had that happen to me."

She stood up quickly, but he rose from the sofa slowly. She was only inches away from him now; the heat from his body enveloped her. It was as though an internal master switch had been thrown to light up every nerve ending within her. Suddenly her skin felt so overly sensitive it ached. Standing in the wake of his intense heat, she felt herself moisten as though her body was trying to put our unseen flames. True hunger crept between her thighs, licking at her swollen, hot flesh. Just as suddenly her nipples tightened, sending pinpoints of stinging need to raise gooseflesh on her arms.

Reason warred with primal instinct. She knew the right thing to do was to step away from this man. Never in her life had anyone had this kind of inexplicable effect on her. Not this fast. Not this intense. She didn't know him, and this was too crazy to consider. But her body was betraying her badly, even if she couldn't fathom why. More damning was the fact that he looked just as bewildered and out of control as she probably did, appearing as though this unnamed thing had blindsided him, too. That silent confession that he offered by his intense gaze, his slightly flaring nostrils each time he took what seemed like a deliberately slowed breath, only raised the stakes of the chemical chain reaction.

"We have to stay focused on the mission . . . and then if we live, we'll see what happens." She bit her bottom lip, hesitating. "But right now you should probably leave."

"Is that what you want?" He waited and stared at her, his gaze making her stomach do flip-flops.

"No," she said just above a whisper. "But that's probably what should happen."

"Yeah . . . That is probably what should happen," he repeated in a deep, sensual rumble.

But neither of them moved as he lowered his mouth to hers and kissed her gently, allowing her to taste black coffee and sugar and freedom and hope. The clean, uncomplicated scent of Ivory soap filled her nose, that and his wonderful male signature blended into it. She deepened the kiss and stepped into his warmth, feeling a pair of strong arms slowly enfold her to block out the cruel, ugly world.

In that fragile moment a promise was cast. He'd come back for her, to serve and protect. Tears of relief spilled down her cheeks. Never in her life had anyone made her feel safe. That had been the catalyst, the trigger that flipped the master switch inside her. No one had ever stepped into that dangerous void to make her feel like he could handle come what may.

That dark place in her soul where hope was a dying light was an amazingly complex place that no average man could occupy. Captain Anthony Davis stepped into the breach with authority.

Her intellectual mind didn't have to know him; she felt this man at the cellular level.

His presence radiated through her being as an honest street warrior, an assassin with swagger, an honorable man with blood on his hands—one versed in dealing death, but who would never hurt an innocent . . . someone who could give her absolution for all her crimes against her own body, mind, and spirit, understanding why she did what she did and still finding something redeeming within her. A man who could still see some innocence left in her battered heart.

This man knew what she did for a living, knew what she did for a cause greater than herself . . . and yet he'd come back for her and had wrapped her in his arms. That shit was so sexy she could barely catch her breath. To clearly be an alpha female and to be able, for once, to look into the eyes of a true alpha male—not a pretender, not a wannabe alpha, but one so secure that he didn't even have to raise his voice or do stupid power plays . . . one who didn't blink or stutter about what he wanted, one who plainly made it clear that he wanted more than her body, wanted the whole package . . . and wasn't afraid of that, either . . . well, just damn . . .

She held on to him tightly. No man that she'd been with had ever known the full extent of her job or what she was capable of; not one of them could deal with her in total. Those who did know, the men she'd worked with all her career, might have wanted her physically, but not as the whole package deal. To them she was just for fun, and since she wasn't playing games with her body or heart, she'd given them neither. Captain Anthony Davis was dangerous in that regard, because he was well within the strike zone of being able to claim both.

This man felt different than all the others before, and if her life depended on it, she couldn't have explained why. Maybe it was a knowing that was loosely connected to the fact that he'd fought her in hand-to-hand combat and had still returned. The way he looked at her told her without words that to him, she wasn't a freak or a conquest or a potential lay on the job; he'd come back to put himself between her and sure harm.

Sage broke their kiss and buried her face against his shoulder. To her surprise, he petted her back and then stroked her hair.

"It's going to be all right, baby," he murmured, which only made the tears come in earnest.

No man had ever told her it was going to be all right in a way that made her believe it. But somehow the confidence in his tone, and having seen what he did for a living, made her know she could bank on whatever this man said.

"Oh, God, what have I gotten myself into?"

She took in a choked breath and allowed her fingers to splay across his back. "I can't even look at myself in the mirror sometimes—and even if I kill that bastard, I don't know if that'll make a difference . . . it won't matter. My Nana was right. There's a line and damn you, Anthony Davis, for making me find it."

A pair of rough, warm hands sought her face and lifted it as the most open gaze met hers.

"Sage . . . let me be your mirror for a little while then, because all I see is a beautiful woman, one with a beautiful heart, who's capable and fearless, and decent and good. In the hospital, I saw it in your eyes—your heart and the toll this was taking on you. Don't ask me how, but I knew you were near this point . . . that's another reason why I came back. I promise you, I'll never leave you in there alone, all right? We'll get this done. We'll get this over. And no matter what happens, nothing you had to do was in vain. You may never know how many lives you've saved by what you did. If nobody else knows that, I do . . . but even more important than that, you have to know it and believe it. Understood?"

She nodded and held onto his thick wrists, needing to feel tangible evidence of his solid presence. He wasn't a dream, wasn't a mirage. He was real and was someone she had to care about.

"I don't let people in because I can't bear it if they die," she whispered, saying the truth out

loud for the very first time. "And when it came
to men in my life, I think I only let in jerks, so if
they burned me, I could live with the loss . . . the
disappointment wasn't that great if they walked
out of my life—which they all eventually did.
Sort of a self-fulfilling prophecy." She let out a
sad sigh and tried to smile. "I told you, I'm really screwed up as a person."

"I let in one person that I trusted and she
burned me with my boy . . . he was stateside, I
was deployed. Let's just say it was a double violation. After that, I vowed I'd never go there again
and I left a trail of very inconsequential hookups
in my wake. I closed people out, too. So we both
have a checkered past, and what?"

His thumbs caressed the edges of her jaw and
he brushed a kiss against the cheekbone that he'd
grazed. "We all have our ways to avoid pain,
Sage. That doesn't make you a bad person, just
human. Then something unexpected happened. I
met you. The timing really sucks. But it is what
it is. The one thing this profession should have
taught us both is, life is short and tomorrow's
not promised. Like I said, I'm not about holding back vital intel from where it needs to be
communicated—and you need to know everything I'm saying to you tonight."

She slid her hands off his wrists to place them
lightly against his stone-cut chest. The gentle
tremor that ran through his fingertips, coupled

with the warmth of his palms, made her face feel like it would literally melt in his hands.

"This isn't just physical attraction."

He shook his head. "No. That wouldn't be scary at all."

"No, it wouldn't."

"That wouldn't have made me fly from New Orleans to be here under circumstances that could compromise our careers, get us both killed, and possibly jeopardize the mission."

She shook her head. "And if it was just that . . . I wouldn't be standing here crying, whispering, and basically freaking out."

"I should probably go," he murmured as the tremor in his hands seemed to wash through his body.

"Is that what you want?" she asked, stepping in closer to allow their bodies to touch.

His stomach tightened brick by glorious brick. "No," he replied in a hoarse whisper and then took her mouth again, but harder this time. "But that's probably what should happen," he murmured into her mouth as soon as their kiss broke. "God help me, that's probably what should happen."

CHAPTER 8

His body ignited as she pressed and writhed against him. Everything female about her imploded in his groin. Hard shaft contractions that were totally beyond his control made his hands tremble as they followed the lush contours of her curves until her breath hitched.

A soft, coffee-laced tongue swept his in a moonlit erotic dance. The scent of a woman, this woman, drilled down past all reason. Her perfume was now imprinted within the primal part of his brain—pure reflex was the only response to it . . . just like her butter soft skin caused delirium. Silken tresses spilled into his hands as he ever so gently cradled her skull, rough pelvic friction a fabric-induced serenade.

Every touch he landed against her skin was done with reverence, an apology for the earlier combat when he didn't know who she was. He wanted her to know that would never happen again under any circumstances. She had to know that he understood the phrase "make love not war" when it came to the female form.

The Creator must have heard his prayers and sent him an angel—someone to restore his battered faith that there was something still worth fighting for, someone in this world beyond his band of brothers who would care or think that he made a difference. Yet, from the way her smooth hands caressed his back and her long, slender fingers threaded through his hair, he could tell she was asking him for forgiveness when all he could do was beg for hers.

How could she know what he couldn't put into words himself? He knew her fatigue, the kind of battle weariness that clawed at one's bones and gristle. It was more than exhaustion, it was the wearing away of the human spirit after witnessing too much gore and violence, only to have that made a mockery by war-profiteering fat cats and politicians, none of whom would know patriotism if it jumped up and bit them.

He and Sage had the same questions. They were both fighting for justice in an unjust world. And both of them were tired and had clearly recognized that in each other's eyes.

Endless battle bred uncommon despair, just as seeing injustice at home and not only abroad bred dangerous questions like, what are we fighting for? She'd no doubt seen abuses in the criminal justice system like he'd seen abuses in the military. It had made him start to wonder who the true enemy was and why the politicians weren't declaring war and spilling the blood of their sons and daughters, too.

As he kissed Sage deeply, he was sure she'd asked herself why justice only seemed to work for the wealthy and why so many kids from the hood seemed to get the harshest sentence. Sage Wagner was cut from the same bolt of cloth that he was sheared from—the old neighborhoods with common sense and a solid moral compass as a guide.

Rhetoric be damned, he needed a woman who understood, whose touch communicated that she did. Inside he'd been trying to figure out what he was doing in the service—why the fat cats' stocks were rising on the Dow and NASDAQ while their buddies were making millions in military contracts, but those with their asses on the line, who'd literally bled for the American dream, were trying to stave off foreclosures?

He kissed Sage harder, seeking answers and redemption in her mouth, washing his mind and hands clean against the soft skin of her back and the wondrous swell of her divinely perfect ass.

Each hard exhale and inhale she caused was a silent pardon, a prayer chant to just make him forget so he could go forth and do his job. But instead of exonerating him, she filled his mouth with a soft moan and made him swallow it, then echo it back. She would give as good as she got—a pardon for a pardon, a mercy for a mercy, a blackout for a blackout ... oh ... God ... yes ...

Didn't she understand that he'd been searching for her all his life—a woman to whom he didn't have to explain what being a soldier meant? The knowing meant freedom; that she still wanted him after comprehending was sexy as all hell.

Not many women, he suspected, and certainly none he'd ever met, knew what it really meant to take a life and then live with that. None he'd ever slept with could imagine what it felt like to day after day, year after year, hunt an enemy that multiplied like cockroaches no matter what you used against them. And how did a man who'd seen too much and lived to tell about it, bring all that home to the suburbs and shopping malls and expect to be normal?

Sage Wagner didn't expect him to be civilian normal. With her, he didn't have to pretend to fit in. That was the true promise of freedom she offered. In her arms were truth, justice, and the American way. She was a warrior and knew down to her marrow what he was. They didn't have to talk about it or analyze it; they just had to live it ... and right now he wanted her so badly that it was almost impossible to breathe.

With that intimate knowledge, her hands

sought his skin to soak up the pain. Her gentle touch anointed his body with healing through pleasure. She was the first responder to his tortured soul. And as his hands slid up her torso beneath her blouse, she released a low, sexy gasp that let him know that he was hers as well.

Only inches from his face, their eyes met as she slowly raised a shapely leg to hook it around his waist. Staring at him, huffing short bursts of warm, moist breath into his mouth, she rode his shaft through his pants, watching him slowly thumb her tight nipples, making them both crazy as she bore down harder like he was already inside her.

They both knew they were playing a dangerous game of chicken to see who would blink first. She lifted his shirt, tugging it free, and allowed her searing touch to fan out across his chest and nipples. The skin on skin contact was too much. He blinked and blinked hard, lifting her up by the tight globes of her ass while thrusting his tongue deep into her mouth.

But when they were halfway to the bedroom, walking blindly, her cell phone rang. They both froze. He set her down, breathing hard. Her eyes cast a warning that she never had to verbalize.

She answered on the fourth ring and made her voice sound sleepy. "Roberto?"

Anthony walked away toward the sofa and rubbed the nape of his neck. Frustration and jealousy made a dangerous cocktail in his bloodstream right now.

"I was asleep," she crooned with a frown, mouthing "I'm sorry."

He just silently nodded, groin throbbing, and wondered how in the hell he'd found himself playing the role of the secondary lover to a drug baron.

"Yeah . . . I miss you, too," she said, rolling her eyes. Then her voice changed and her expression became pained. "Baby . . . I'm tired . . . yeah, I miss you, too, but I don't feel like it right now. Come on, I'll see you soon, right?"

Jealousy bristled the hair on the nape of Anthony's neck, and yet this was a part of the mission. He forced chivalry into his eyes and nodded at her and then motioned to the door. She nodded and blew him a kiss, mouthing "thank you" and "I'm sorry." He quietly collected his gun and slipped into the adjoining room and shut the door behind him with a soft click.

Of course a man as paranoid as Roberto Salazar would do a bed check on his woman. Made sense, who was he fooling? Not to mention, being away from her could be eased by some late-night phone sex. What red-blooded man in his right mind wouldn't want to call Sage like that? But the entire situation just kicked his ass.

Anthony allowed the gun to dangle by his side for a moment, defeated. It didn't help matters that the erection she'd left him with needed immediate attention. And as much as he hated who she was on the phone with, knowing that she was probably in the next room with her hand between her lovely legs was driving him insane.

The mental picture was vivid. If he trusted himself enough not to make a sound, which he didn't, right now he was so far gone that if she asked him to, he'd get on his knees at the edge of her bed and taste her till she screamed whatever on her cell. Once she got that crazy bastard off her phone, he'd finish her off hard and long.

The fantasy made another wave of desire crawl through his heavy groin. He briefly closed his eyes as a shudder of want washed through him. Damn . . .

Anthony shook his head and banished the thought, then pushed off the wall, left his gun on the TV cabinet, and headed to the bathroom for a towel. A light, feminine tap at his door stopped him mid-step. He swallowed hard and then rushed over to open it. She was standing there, chewing her bottom lip, eyes troubled. The combination was so sexy that he forgot to breathe.

"I'm sorry. I got him off the phone as fast as I could . . . and I know—"

His kiss crushed her mouth, stopping the awkward apology. He didn't want her to say another word. Whatever she'd had to say or do to get rid of Salazar was on a need-to-know basis, and he damned sure didn't need to know right now.

The important point was, she'd come back for him. This wasn't sloppy seconds in the least. The way he saw it, Salazar had interrupted them. He didn't care whatever bullshit she had to say to their enemy to get him off her phone as quickly as she did. She came back for him.

Her hands covered his ass, pulling him against her, thanking him in friction for not damning her for just doing her job. Careful not to mark her skin, he spilled kisses down the side of her neck, paying homage to the goddess of mercy that she had returned. She rewarded him by stripping off her blouse and bra, leaving him so in awe that for a moment all he could do was stare as her breasts bounced from the royal blue fabric.

Pretty caramel nipples called his name, begging for his mouth with their taut pout. Her head tilted back, she breathed through her barely parted lips and moaned without censor as his tongue grazed her pebbled skin.

The sound told him she was still on fire and nothing that had happened on the phone had quenched her. Maybe she hadn't cum for Salazar and had just gotten him off alone, making pretend like phone sex operators did while painting their nails . . . or maybe she'd just talked trash to the guy while really thinking of him. He hated to admit it, but it did make a small difference. An important one.

Slipping a hand deep into her pants confirmed his theory. Warm, wet, folds of swollen heat met his fingers as her grip tightened on his shoulders. Before he could shimmy her pants down, she bucked against his hand, locking it between their pelvises, holding him by the back of his shirt. Her breath said emergency; she needed release now and couldn't wait. Her grimace and tempo was the meter for how close she was, edging him closer to insanity with her.

Suddenly she cried out against his chest, muffling the sound in his shirt. Her thighs crushed his palm as her cave sucked his fingers, rhythmically pumping more slickness down them. He wanted to replace them so badly, wished he could feel that same squeezing wet heat flow down his shaft.

Spent, she collapsed against him, her sweet pussy weeping into his hand, while her fingers quickly began unfastening his pants. He kissed the crown of her head, almost in tears himself as she released him. The second her hands captured him, an elongated moan bubbled up from his depths and his hips began to thrust without consulting his brain.

It had been so damned long, so unconnected

and unfulfilling when he'd coupled with unknown women on the road. Then it was just about meeting a physical need, but this . . . this . . . oh, shit, this was going to take his mind.

"Tell me where they are?" she murmured hoarsely, rubbing him against her bare, hot belly.

"I don't know," he said, his voice raw and gasping, just needing her to make the pain stop. "I'm not sure of the target's location." At the moment, if she'd asked for the nuclear missile codes, he would have given them to her if he'd had them.

She stopped moving and kissed him hard, then drew back. "Condoms. You have condoms, right?"

He blinked twice, still breathing hard. "Damn . . ."

She smiled and petted his cheek. "You packed a semi with a full magazine, I bet, several pistols, explosives . . . but that key item wasn't on the artillery list."

He hung his head, resting his forehead against hers. She didn't have to say it; she'd been with Salazar without protection.

But the thing he loved about her was that she didn't make him say out loud what they both knew to be true. Her gentle stroke became tighter and harder, just like his breaths returned harder and stronger, matching his thrusts, matching his heartbeat. He gripped her shoulders, slickening her belly with his increased need until his entire body convulsed against her.

He leaned against her, half braced on the wall, half holding himself up. Beads of sweat rolled down his temples as he sucked in and released huge inhalations of air. Her soft kiss on his cheek let him know, again, that she understood and wasn't upset. Her blouse was no doubt ruined, but her gentle strokes were calm and comforting now, as though to say, it was all right.

"I'm sorry," he murmured. "I . . ."

"Didn't know any more than I did that this would happen."

He nodded. "Yeah. I definitely wasn't prepared."

"In this case, I think that's kind of sweet, actually. You brought me a gun and not a condom. Makes a girl feel appreciated and not taken for granted."

He could feel her smile against his shoulder and the absurdity of their lives made him chuckle.

She looked up at him, seeming not quite sure what to do with her wet hands and soiled blouse. "You owe me one, Captain."

"I'll definitely replace the blouse," he said, suddenly feeling the full sting of embarrassment. "And, uh, let me get you a towel."

"Stand down, man," she said sweetly, and then

nipped his ear. She pulled back with a big smile. "I meant you owe me a full frontal offensive, full metal jacket . . . later . . . if you catch my drift." She leaned into him and sent a sexy message into his ear, making his body stir again. "You can take the beach, the hill, or whatever you want, Captain Anthony Davis. Later. All right?"

"Roger that," he murmured into her ear and then kissed her again. He wanted to wake up next to this woman—correction—he wanted to go get a twelve box of Magnums, return to the room, and make love to Sage Wagner until they both passed out, and *then* wake up next to her. But as she backed up and nodded toward the door with a mischievous, sexy grin, he knew their interlude was over for now.

"Would a soldier mind opening a door for a lady? We'd better get some shut-eye. Tomorrow, who knows what we'll be facing."

CHAPTER 9

She'd slept like the dead and woken up with a slight headache, but within a few moments of awareness, the prior night came flooding back to her, making her smile.

Thrusting herself out of bed, she saw no way to avoid the inevitable. Roberto would be back within the next twenty-four to forty-eight hours, and she had to steel herself for that eventuality. He hadn't taken her sleepy rebuff very well, especially when she'd feigned nodding off in the midst of his crude attempt at phone sex. The process took some linguistic dexterity that the man didn't own, not because he was unintelligent, but because he was unimaginative and, worse yet, selfish. So a megalomaniac wouldn't know what kinds of imagery got a woman off. More important, he had never bothered to learn what got her off, and it was very obvious that he didn't care.

Regardless, it didn't matter. He wasn't her lover, even if he was temporarily her problem. Salazar could tell the boys in prison to fuck him and suck him, because where he was going, he was going to have to use plenty of imagination to do his hard time.

She tightened the sash on the white, terry hotel robe she'd slept in as she crossed the room, and then froze when she saw two coffee cups. Bad move. Hurrying over to them, she quickly collected the mugs and rinsed them out, and returned one dry one to where it had been. Mistakes like that could cost lives. Damn. She had to get her head back in the game.

Checking her damp blouse in the bathroom, she used the hair dryer to finish the job on it, as well as on her bra, panties, and pants that she'd hand-washed in the sink the night before. Then she quickly stashed it in a hotel laundry bag and tagged it for housekeeping. At least half of her brain was still working.

Rushing back into the bedroom, she checked her cell phone again. Good. No news was good news.

He woke up with his body saluting him, thinking of Sage. He closed his eyes again for a moment once he'd glimpsed the tented sheet and then forced himself to sit up. Taking a whiz with an erection was a pain in the ass, and no matter what had happened last night, today he had to be sharp. Anything could go down at any minute.

His cell phone vibrating on the nightstand was exactly that something he'd been expecting. When he clicked answer, Lieutenant Hayes's voice filled the line on this encrypted cell.

"Captain, we just got word that Agent Alvarez is going to do your introduction to Salazar today. All of his key North American distributors are going to meet up at a French Quarter gated mansion he owns in New Orleans later tonight. Agent Alvarez will be going by Rene Santiago, and he'll stash cash, clothes, and a kitted-up BMW 735i for you at the Hotel Monteleone."

"I copy. But what about the arms dealer?"

"Word is, some type of activity will be coming into one of Canada's eastern ports two days from now, so until then Assad and Salazar will be joined at the hip. The details of that transaction are still unclear."

"Roger that, Lieutenant."

Anthony disconnected the call and got out of bed. He tapped on the adjoining door and was rewarded a few moments later by Sage's radiant smile. She only had a robe on; he had slept in his boxers.

"Man . . . I wish I could stay and have breakfast with you . . . or have you for breakfast, but I've gotta go."

Her smile slowly faded, but it never became

desolate. "I wish we could, too, but hey." She sighed and hugged herself. "So fill me in."

She nodded and kissed him gently. "You be careful, Juan . . . all right?"

He nodded and caressed her face. "I'm coming back to you, Camille. Believe that."

"I don't like this at all, Roberto." Hector looked at his brother as the maid set down breakfast before them. He waited until she was out of earshot and glanced around the French Quarter mansion that was their temporary compound in the city. "The Mexicans are coming across the border towns in the southwest . . . bold, like Colombians were back home. Killing entire police departments, wiping out ranches, and they will soon have a cartel here as strong as ours."

"That's why we have to move quickly. The old man doesn't understand that the Mexican families are as hungry as ours used to be. That hunger is dangerous. He is insulated by all that he's built in Colombia. Here in the US, free enterprise rules . . . and perhaps we are not as competitive as we used to be, *sí*?"

"But if we do this thing, we'll no longer have Guzman's guns at our backs as protection. They'll be at our backs as a firing squad. That's why we pay a little more to buy from him—it's an insurance fee, if you think of it that way."

"His insurance fee is not covering the daily expenses of having to protect our distributors in Los Angeles, Arizona, and Nevada!" Roberto said, slamming his fist on the table and making the fine china rattle. "Right now, the pressure is on our people to doubly arm themselves against Mexicans who hope to eat into our territory—and there's the not-so-small issue of lower prices coming from Mexico driving down profits here in the US. Doing the deal with Assad is progress, globalization. Period."

"Guzman will not see this as progress, brother. He will see this as betrayal. Then we will be fighting a war on two fronts and can fall, leaving the strongest members of the Mexican cartel to step right in and stand on our dead bodies."

Roberto Salazar took a forceful bite of sausage from his fork. "You worry too much. It is done now, anyway. In a few days we will double our wealth and army of mercenaries. Then, we will be too strong for Guzman to outright challenge and we can negotiate to form a stronger, more mutually beneficial alliance the way wise businessmen do."

Hector stared at his brother, who'd continued eating. "That's just it—our men will be mercenaries. The Mexican alliances are made up of family . . . blood. Never forget the blood is stronger."

Roberto set down his knife and fork very carefully and took up his napkin to wipe his mouth. With the speed of a cobra's strike, he backhanded his brother, drawing blood when the huge diamond pinky ring he wore gashed Hector's lip.

"Our family died throughout the wars . . . never forget the sacrifice. Colombians were all family once, too—and still betrayed one another, still stabbed each other in the back for power and money. Do not become weak with nostalgia, brother. Superstition and nostalgia keep men believing in ghosts and fairy tales. There is only one common denominator—cash. That is what is king!"

Roberto stood and pushed away from the table, staring down at his cowering brother. "Now is not the time for doubts. The time to speak freely and clearly was when this plan was being formed. Now at the eleventh hour, you have doubts?"

"No, brother . . . just cautions—things you should be aware of."

Nodding, Roberto slowly sat and settled himself. "Of all people, I cannot have you doubt me. You know how much I hate betrayal. Please do not break my heart, Hector."

After the news she'd received from Anthony, she expected the call from Bruno to shortly follow it—and it did. She was to go with Bruno back to the compound, pack enough clothes for a week, and be ready to catch the private jet to New Orleans tomorrow.

Sage pulled her freshly shampooed hair up into a twist and clipped it, touched up her lip gloss, and strode out the front door. The valets would have her little red Merc, but she could pick that up when she got back from the gym. In her locker there she had another encrypted cell that she could use to call her boss, thus closing the intel loop.

Making sure she kept up appearances, she looked both ways before she entered the hall with her shopping bags and then hurried to the stairs. Taking the steps two at a time, she rushed to the seventh floor from the second floor, and then stopped to catch her breath when she reached the right level.

Bruno would be waiting for her in the lobby. He needed to see one of the elevators descend from the floor she was supposed to be on. Dashing down the hall once the coast was clear, she pressed the elevator button and waited, then got on when it opened.

Soon this would all be over, she told herself as the doors opened to the lobby. As expected, Bruno got up. The other security men stood up with him as she sashayed to the front desk and checked out.

"Thank you so much," she said, waiting for the receipt. Turning to Bruno, she smiled at him as though she hadn't a care in the world. "How'd you sleep?"

To her surprise, he smiled back. "Never better."

She gave him a wink and that made him chuckle. "I'm going to put these in the trunk while I go to the gym across the street." Before his smile could completely vanish in protest, she offered him a lovely compromise. "I cannot allow my ass to get fat. Roberto isn't having it, and I didn't do a thing yesterday. So why don't you fellas have breakfast . . . if you feel like you must, one of you can walk me across the street, Geez Louise. But I'll ask the valets to bring my car around so I can put all my shopping bags in the trunk, all right?"

"All right," Bruno muttered, clearly not thrilled about her plan but seeming okay with the breakfast part of it. "How long do you think you'll be?"

"Oh, just an hour, then give me a half to get a shower and get dressed, then I'll stop being a pain in your butt."

That coaxed a new smile out on his face. "Promise me."

She laughed and walked away toward valet parking with a jumble of shopping bags and her receipt.

Tapping her foot, nerves wire-taut, she waited for the valets to bring around her car. Bruno stood by her side patiently, and then walked her across the street without incident. The moment she was in the gym, she greeted the staff and swept by them to find her locker, got a call off to Hank with the update, and then changed into the fresh gear that she had in there.

An hour run on the treadmill did her good, so did another half hour of lifting weights. The workout helped lift the stress and clear her mind. She had to get Anthony out of her head.

Back in a pair of black linen slacks, her black heels, and white linen tank, she donned her designer shades and hoisted her purse and gym bag over her shoulder. Bruno was across the street with her red coupe waiting. Two of his men were smoking. One of the security vehicles was on the parking circle in front of her car, one empty one was behind it. She stepped aside for the cab that came up into the driveway. But what happened next unfolded in slow motion.

Two businessmen and the cabbie got out of the cab that now blocked the first security vehicle and opened fire on Bruno, hitting him at point-blank range in the chest. The silenced bullet ripped through Bruno's body, sending blood splatter against the pristine walls, glass windows, and stone entrance. Before his body hit the ground, the other businessman and cab driver fired two quick shots in the heads of the two smokers. Screams echoed throughout the hotel lobby as guests, valets, and bellmen dove for cover.

Men in the first vehicle that was blocked by the cab panicked, rammed the cab, and then backed up, hitting her coupe. But the second they tried to roll down their windows to open fire, the vehicle exploded as though on a timer, killing them.

Sage's weapon was out of her purse as soon as the first shot was fired. Running toward the scene, she caught the cabbie in the skull before he had a chance to unload a clip on Agent Jennings, who ran right into the firefight looking for her.

"Get down, Dan!" she screamed, running toward him, firing directly at the fleeing hit men.

Agents McCoy and Whittaker kept on enough pressure, firing from a hunkered down position in the lobby, so that the two hit men ran back to the discarded SUV and jumped in it, careening away.

"You all right?" she asked, breathlessly, stooping to check on Dan.

He looked up and nodded, and then brushed himself off as he stood.

She grabbed him by the chest. "Don't ever do that again! You could have been killed—last night I gave you a direct order to fall back and get out of here!"

"But something was wrong!" he shouted. "Somebody had to watch your back, Sage!"

"Gimme your encrypted cell," she said, yanking it out of his hand as he produced it. "And a clip." Sage held out her hand. "Now!"

Agents McCoy and Whittaker were up and running toward her.

"Don't do it, Wagner," Agent McCoy shouted as Sage jumped into the coupe and peeled away from the curb.

Seconds counted, and she'd lost too many of them already. She could still see Bruno's black Durango weaving in and out of traffic erratically as it headed toward the highway. In a situation where size mattered, she had the advantage of speed and German engineering.

The chase was on. She had to find out if these were Colombians or possibly a part of Assad's army that had decided to clean up the American trail left behind their arms deal, now that they had their cash. Just as important, she had to call Anthony. He was no doubt in the air and needed to know that South Beach just blew.

Ten rings and no pickup and no voice mail. Frustration claimed her as she tried to drive at an insane speed and then called Hank.

"Put a chopper in the air, Hank," she said. "I've got two unidentifieds in a hijacked black Durango headed back toward the Salazar compound, of all places."

A crazy swerve on the road and a tractor trailer near miss made her drop the phone. She never heard Hank's message to fall back. Slammed from behind by an F-150 pickup truck, she realized that the men with Uzis hanging out the window weren't trying to shoot her, but rather wanted to capture her.

Shooting at them on an open civilian highway might look good in the movies, but was out of the question in real practice. Families were driving, teenagers were driving, truckers just trying to deliver goods and do their jobs were driving . . . minivans with car seats passed her, car windows containing dogs with their tongues hanging out were beside her. Sage pulled off of the highway and headed toward the Salazar compound. She had to take this firefight away from the public and get the hit men on familiar ground.

But halfway down the road, speeding at 110 mph, she saw the compound and yacht blow up. She hit the brakes, but the F-150 clipped her back bumper as she tried to slow down, sending her into a crazy tailspin with airbags deployed.

Not wearing a seatbelt, she almost went airborne. Before she could reorient herself and find her weapon, three big brutes with Uzis jumped out of the Ford and surrounded her. In rapid sequence, their heads exploded from sniper fire from a source unknown.

Sage was out of the vehicle in seconds, snatched one of the Uzis, and headed for cover. The Durango came out of nowhere and a click at the back of her skull made her decide not to spray it.

"Drop it or die."

A rough hand pulled her behind a tree. She could hear sniper fire exploding wood and car metal, then everything went dark as burlap got yanked over her head. Lifted off her feet and walked slowly forward, she knew she'd just been turned into a human body shield.

Not enough had been said to allow her to pick up an accent. A hard shove pushed her into a vehicle that, judging by the floor and space, had to be a van. Hundreds of questions swirled in her throbbing head as her hands and legs were bound by nylon electrical ties.

Which side was this that held her, and what was the point? Keeping her alive had to be leverage against Salazar—that had to be the only reason. Shit. Snipers had tried to assist; was it DEA or DELTA? Had to be DELTA; they were the only ones with the codes to blow the mansion, compound buildings, and marina. But why? Had to be enough bodies on the premises to make it worth their while . . . or maybe they had a new strategy in play. If so, did Anthony know? He was about to walk right into a hornets' nest in New Orleans! Then there was the not-so-small issue of her now being a hostage. Please, God, if they were going to kill her, just let it be quick.

Damn, damn, damn, it wasn't supposed to go down like this!

CHAPTER 10

Anthony stepped out of Agent Alvarez's silver Lamborghini, wearing clothes that cost more than his monthly salary. They'd been dark for over an hour. He didn't like it.

The warehouse district was perfect for an ambush. Salazar wanted to meet here, but they weren't near his Key West Construction warehouses blocks away. Agent Alvarez, aka Rene Santiago, had been summoned to appear before Salazar at one of his Largo Food warehouses. If Anthony passed inspection, then he'd walk out alive. If not, both he and Alvarez were dead men walking.

But if they didn't come out, nobody was coming out. His DELTA unit, and the DEA agents were lying low in an area holding pattern. Right now enough firepower was focused on the Largo Food warehouse to leave a smoking black hole if anything went down wrong. The combined units had been instructed not to rush in if a couple early shots were fired, as that gun report could be nothing more than a few testing shots— just some rounds clicked off to intimidate a new guy being brought before the boss. If all hell broke loose or they didn't come out in the Lamborghini, then and only then were the units to move in on that warehouse and the Key West Construction warehouses.

Two burly guards patted them down and confiscated their weapons as they waited for Roberto to appear. Anthony's nerves twitched silently beneath his skin as his sunglass-shielded gaze traveled along the warehouse catwalks, shelves, and huge pallets of inventory. The guards had handheld Uzis; five more men scattered throughout the quiet shipping floor had gats. Seven visible enemy combatants. Anthony remained cool, waiting, looking for anything that could be used as a weapon, should he need it.

A rusty nail on the floor could kill a man. An abandoned crowbar used for opening crates was a sure instrument of death. Deep aisles filled with inventory were a diversionary shield. A discarded ink pen could end a man's life. And all of it was within his reach, making him feel slightly better.

The entrance guards carrying Uzis had their guns lowered now. Interior guards hadn't drawn theirs yet, just flashed them. In a true firefight, it would take a few seconds for information to register to the human brain and for them to react—it was within those few fragile seconds that the men of DELTA Force had been trained to kill.

Standing wide-legged, relaxed, left hand clasping his right wrist and flashing a platinum Rolex, Anthony waited next to Agent Alvarez. Soon multiple footfalls echoed in the warehouse. No one moved, so he knew it had to be Salazar accompanied by two more men. The hunch paid off as tense guards nodded a greeting to the boss.

"So, Rene . . . this is your cousin?"

"*Sí*, Roberto. Juan Morales. The cops—"

"Yes, I know—they took our man down for some domestic bullshit." Roberto Salazar shook his head and glanced at the two men that flanked him. One was Assad with a Beretta out and cocked. He'd know that gaunt face and lanky frame anywhere. The other looked like a slimmer, shorter version of Roberto—had to be Hector. "This is why I always tell you, follow the law. Pay your fucking traffic tickets and your taxes. Don't even jaywalk, and pay your bitches child support or whatever, because it interferes with business."

Roberto nodded toward the Lamborghini behind them and then focused on Agent Alvarez.

"Like what the fuck is that, Rene? In Los Angeles, okay. But coming south with New York tags . . . are you insane?"

Alvarez hung his head. "I'll get rid of it, Roberto."

Ignoring him, Roberto motioned to Anthony to step forward.

"Take off the glasses. I need to look into a man's eyes to know what's in his soul."

Anthony took off his shades, carefully put them in the breast pocket of his Armani suit, and stepped up to stand two feet in front of Roberto. Their eyes met. Neither blinked as they appraised each another. Pure outrage passed through Anthony. He wanted to kill Roberto so badly for the pain he'd caused Sage that it was all he could do to remain motionless. A woman stood between them in more ways than one.

"This motherfucker's got heart," Roberto finally announced. "My own brother cannot look me in the eye like that." He glanced over to Hector. "But a man with too much heart is a dangerous thing, especially in times of uncertainty like we're living in today." He then looked at Assad. "You and I have seen eye to eye since the beginning."

Assad nodded. "A man who is not afraid to die is a dangerous thing or a blessing, depending on whose side he's on."

A high shadow moved in Anthony's peripheral vision. When he spun to meet it, the sniper jerked, revealing his position for a flash. He wasn't wearing fatigues; it wasn't one of his. Hair-trigger reflexes kicked in, and Anthony grabbed Assad's hand with the gun still in it, kicked Roberto out of the way of the shot coming from the shelves, and squeezed the trigger. Two seconds later, the entire warehouse erupted in booming voices as the shooter fell forward to his death onto the floor.

Anthony and Assad were face to face. He'd stripped Assad of his gun and was walking toward the body. It couldn't have been one of Roberto's men, because they wouldn't have risked trying to shoot a newcomer that close to the VIPs. Instant logic dictated that, if they'd wanted him dead, Roberto was the kind of control freak who would have enjoyed making him get on his knees before unloading a shell in his head. It couldn't have been DELTA or DEA, they'd been instructed to hold and lie low, and *none* of them were to be inside the warehouse to risk a tip-off. No. This was an intruder.

All guns were on Anthony as he walked over to the body and kicked the rifle away from it, then fired a shot in the back of the man's head. Three shots had been fired now, a rifle shot plus two from a Beretta, and he had to only pray that his men's nerves would hold. Right now was not the time for a rescue raid. Not yet.

"You know this bastard?" Anthony shouted, kicking the dead man's body over with his foot.

Roberto dusted himself off and drew near as the confused guards gathered around with weapons pointed at Anthony and Alvarez. He slapped their extended guns down.

"A new man walks into my warehouse and saves my life, my brother's life, and my new client's life and you slow bitches didn't even see this coming!" Roberto spun in a crazed circle, spittle flying as he shouted. "What do I pay you for?"

"I recognize this man," Hector said, visibly shaken. He glanced around the group and then allowed his gaze to settle on his brother's wild eyes. "This man is from Colombia."

Pure silence ricocheted throughout the warehouse. Assad broke it with shattering calm as Anthony bowed and returned his gun to him, handle first.

"I have delivered the product, you have paid me," Assad said in a matter-of-fact tone. "Your men will be here tonight to set the terms of your distribution so you can in turn make money from our arrangement . . . and I need my arms delivered in Canada without further incident. If there is a war brewing between you and your original supplier, that is not our affair. That, as you say, is a domestic problem inside your house. My brothers and I are fighting a war on a much different front for Allah. I hope you understand."

"Completely understood," Roberto said. "This does not change the arrangement regarding the weapons."

"Good," Assad replied, staring at Anthony. "As I said—a man who is not afraid to die can be a blessing, if he is fighting on your side. It appears this Mr. Morales is such a man with good eyes and quick hands. I should like to see him close to us as we complete our transactions over the next several days."

"Done," Roberto said, staring at Anthony. He motioned to his guards, who seemed to instinctively know to give Anthony and Alvarez their guns back. "You've just earned yourself a rank promotion. Go collect your things and have Rene bring you to the house early. But, Rene, do not arrive at my house in that cop magnet vehicle, either."

"*Sí*, Jefe," Alvarez said, keeping his gaze cast low.

Anthony nodded as he holstered his weapon beneath his jacket.

"I should like to return to my hotel," Assad said, glancing at Roberto. "I cannot be anywhere near this. I will see you at dinner."

Roberto nodded and spoke to his men. "Two-man detail—take our client back to Harrah's. Clean up this mess." He began walking as Assad withdrew, and spoke to Anthony and Alvarez over his shoulder.

"Santiago—you are cleared to bring Juan in to the family meeting in the French Quarter tonight."

There was no more to be said as Roberto took a call on his cell and disappeared into the aisles. Bulky guards dragged the dead man away and slung him into the back of a parked Largo Food van. This time there was no escort as he and Alvarez got into the Lamborghini. Both men remained quiet as they backed out of the warehouse, passed by secret checkpoints so their men could see that they'd made it out alive, and entered the construction-gravel laden streets that would ultimately lead to the highway.

They waited until they were on the open road, visibly clear of Roberto's men, before either said a word.

"Holy Christ!" Alvarez exclaimed once in normal traffic. He ran his fingers through his hair. "I didn't even see that coming. I just dove for the floor, figured you had snapped and were about to pull some crazy Rambo shit! Then once the shot got fired, I was expecting a chain reaction that would bring down hellfire from our teams. How'd you see that, man?"

"I told you, Colombians had been spotted on the cargo ship. I knew they'd be gunning for Salazar, and the setup didn't make sense. All his men on the ground had a clear shot at us. Why would some dude take a risky shot to hide and try to hit us, when one of the guards on the ground could have easily popped us at point-blank range? Hide, for what? It wasn't like we had visible backup in there that they had to worry about, right?"

"True, true," Alvarez said, wiping his brow.

"If anything, they would have played with us and intimidated us, not had a hidden sniper to kill us so the shot came without us seeing it. The whole goal of terrorism is to terrify. A quick shot you never see coming isn't anything but merciful."

"Damn ... okay, you've got a point. But, man ... how in the hell did you figure all that out in three seconds?"

"I wasn't trying to figure it out in three seconds. I started placing the pieces on the chessboard from the moment I saw how the board was set up when we drove in and got out of the car."

Alvarez extended his fist toward Anthony's and pounded it. "Glad to have one of the dudes who gets more done by five A.M. than most people get done in a week on our team."

"Thanks for bringing me in, man. Took balls to stand there in front of Salazar with a long story."

"We try," Alvarez said with a half smile. "But we're gonna have to change cars and go to his house in yours. This was the flyest thing I could get out of the impound lot. Reach under the dashboard and feel for duct tape. My encrypted cell is mounted there. This is a need-to-know incident back at headquarters, especially since you just got promoted into the inner circle."

Following Alvarez's instructions, Anthony felt beneath the dashboard until his hand came into contact with the taped-down cell phone. Once he'd recovered it, he stared at the display.

"You've got a lot of missed calls, man."

Alvarez accepted the phone and hit a speed dial button. "Talk to me people. We're still alive," he said quickly as soon as the call connected. His eyes widened and he glanced at Anthony several times. "Damn it!" He punched the dashboard and pressed the phone to his ear. "Yeah, well add this to the list: Captain Davis just took down a Colombian family sniper—yeah, one of Guzman's men, at the Largo Food warehouse. That's earned him a promotion. Assad trusts him now, and so does Roberto ... he actually saved Roberto's life, so he's in good. We'll find her. Tell Hank, we'll find her, all right. Yeah. Bye."

"What happened?" Anthony took the phone out of Alvarez's hand and began dialing his unit. A sick feeling clawed at his gizzard as he waited for the call to connect and for Alvarez to speak.

"They got Agent Wagner," Alvarez said, eyes blazing. "A clusterfuck happened in Miami.

Bruno and his men got ambushed, the house was—"

"Hold it," Anthony shouted, going to his connected call. "Lieutenant—what the fuck, over?"

"We had to blow the compound to cover our tracks," Lieutenant Hayes said quickly. "The Colombians came in and murdered Salazar's home security team at his compound . . . just overran the place, sir. They were staking it out and lying in wait for Salazar's men to bring Special Agent Wagner there, where we can only assume they were planning to abduct her. We were in the hold pattern you'd established, sir, and just watching them—when one of them found a DEA bug. That started a whole grounds search and they found a military C4 brick behind the drainpipe in the back of the house. We had fifty Colombians onsite, with maybe ten to fifteen of Salazar's men. You had gone dark, sir. The colonel gave the order to blow the grounds to keep a call from going out that could alert the enemy and jeopardize the mission."

"Damn!" Anthony pounded the door with the side of his fist. "What is the status of Special Agent Wagner?"

"We lost her, sir."

"What the hell do you men you lost her, Lieutenant? Clarify!"

"She'd taken down a shooter at the hotel,

one of the three combatants that killed five of
Salazar's men—and from there was involved in
a high-speed chase with a Durango and an F-150
that made it almost to the grounds as we blew the
compound, sir. We trained our sniper fire on the
two vehicles that boxed her in after the impact
of the blast. We got a couple of them, sir. But we
lost some visibility due to billowing smoke, and
the choppers had to navigate around it. That took
our eye off the ball and we lost a visual for several
minutes. But we followed both black vans, and
DEA and local authorities went after the Largo
Food van that emerged onto the road and out of
the smoke a half mile away. Helicopters got to
the warehouse, but by then, ten eighteen-wheelers
had left the garages. We couldn't tell which one to
follow, sir. We set up roadblocks for all Largo
Food trucks and vans. She wasn't in the Largo van
or the black vans, sir."

Anthony rubbed his hand down his face. "Keep
me posted, Lieutenant," he said as calmly as he
could. "Out."

Alvarez looked at him. "It's the Colombians
that have her, isn't it?"

Anthony nodded.

"Fuck me," Alvarez murmured and briefly
closed his eyes. "They think she's Salazar's woman,
and for the double-cross, will send him mental
torture tapes showing them doing God only

knows what to her, body parts . . . you know how this works, man."

"If I have to go to Colombia myself and meet with Guzman, I'm gonna get her back before any of that happens." Anthony kept his gaze on the road before him. "We never leave our own—and I *definitely* never leave mine."

CHAPTER 11

The sound of gunshots rang in her ears, then suddenly the vehicle she was in felt like it had collided with something solid. Banging, tumbling, her body hit seats and interior walls with a thud as the bone-grating sounds of metal scraping against metal burned into her consciousness. Then just as suddenly her body was wrested from the dark confines and smoke filled her nose.

Coughing and sputtering, she was flung into another vehicle. Once again, the brightness that had peeked through the knap of the burlap went dark as a door slammed above her. Wheezing, she tried to get her bearings to no avail. But this time the space was smaller, tighter, and what felt like a wheel was at her back. Instinct told her she was in a trunk. She used that knowledge to calm herself as she tried to feel around for anything behind her that she could use to cut the nylon ties. Unfortunately, she came away wanting. The trunk was clean and the car had a new car smell to it.

After a long time, the vehicle stopped, bright light danced through the burlap again, and her body was lifted up and out of its enclosure. To her surprise, the burlap was gently pulled up and over her head. She stood face-to-face with Rico, Bruno's second-in-command. Dirty tears streaked his face as he stared at her.

"It's all gone, Señorita . . ." He swallowed hard and shook his head. "Forgive me for having to take you like this, but it was the only way to keep you safe. The Colombians . . ."

He cut away the nylon ties at her hands and feet, and then stood, assessing her. "Are you hurt?"

Still partly in shock, she shook her head no and allowed tears of relief to spill down her cheeks. His shirt was bloody and she could see that he'd been shot in the arm. When she looked at his wound, he wiped his brow with the back of his forearm.

"Just grazed. I'm lucky to be alive, so are you. We have to hurry. It's too hot to get you out of Miami right now. I drove to West Palm Beach where Roberto has arranged for a private charter. The hacienda is gone. Bruno is dead. A lot of good men died today. They blew up the entire place . . . the yacht. You have to be with Roberto now to be safe."

"What's happening, Rico?" she whispered. Staying in character wasn't hard. She'd been traumatized, bodily shaken, and seeming upset was no stretch.

He shook his head. "I've said too much already, even mentioning Colombians. *Por favor,* if you care anything about me, don't let Roberto know I said that. Say . . . say you overhead one of the killers mention that, if you must. But right now, I have to get us on that flight, *comprende?*"

Anthony sat in a gold silk-embroidered Louis the XIX chair at the table next to Agent Alvarez, facing Roberto and Hector Salazar before an outrageous buffet of Cajun shrimp, jambalaya, crabmeat, spicy rice and beans, étouffé, and a variety of salads, along with carved lamb and barbecued beef brisket. Security guards toting heavy artillery were strategically posted around the outer doors of the huge dining room. Highly polished, sixteenth-century mahogany winked through the hand-crocheted lace tablecloth as a bottle of Dom Perignon was opened and poured.

Roberto waited until the flutes were filled and the server had left the four men alone. He lifted his glass. "To new alliances."

Anthony lifted his glass and waited to sip from it until Roberto had.

"Eat," Roberto ordered the men at the table. "This is a wake. We've lost much, but will have it replaced tenfold. Some of what happened could not be avoided. But we are still standing."

A terrible sinking feeling twisted in Anthony's gut as he put a few shrimp on his plate.

"I lost many good men today," Roberto said, not speaking to anyone in particular as he sloppily helped himself to the various dishes on the table. He stopped and looked at Anthony's small helping. "A man who knows not to appear too greedy. I like that," he said, nodding and sending a chastising glance toward Alvarez and his brother. "But we grew up poor, *si*? I vowed to never know hunger again, even on my last day alive if it should come to that . . . so I give you permission to eat your fill here at my table as my new head of security."

Hector choked on his sip of champagne. "But we do not know this man?"

"I know that Bruno is dead. I know that this man saved my life and was willing to take a bullet for me and you. Our men could have gotten the wrong impression when he went for Assad's gun and blown his head off—but he was focused on the shooter that none of us saw. That is why he has earned the right to that title and can sit here now with you and me. His cousin," he added, waving toward Alvarez, "is here out of respect because he brought me his family and made a good recommendation, even if his flashy car was unwise. Juan Morales was a good decision . . .

and I reward the good and punish the bad. It is the law in the family."

Hector eyed Anthony and then lowered his gaze and began eating in disgruntled silence. Anthony picked up a shrimp and ate it quietly, hating to have to waste time here with Salazar when Assad was out there and, more important, Sage was in the hands of barbarians. He knew his unit was all over tailing Assad, but no one had a bead on Sage.

"They blew up my home," Roberto said in a too calm tone while still eating. He spoke as though he was discussing the weather. That was when Anthony truly decided he was mad. "I lost perhaps twenty . . . maybe twenty-five good men today. The property can be replaced. I had insurance for that and the yacht . . . boats . . . cars . . . and will have county inspectors paid to blame it on a gas main. I still have favors on the police force, and they'll collect all the shells and make things tidy. These good men at my home, unfortunately, lost their lives because they had eaten too well from my table and had gotten soft. Madre de Dios rest Bruno's soul."

Roberto continued his litany waving a jumbo shrimp, using it to emphasize his erratic point. "Just like I had these imported because the Gulf is poisoned, you can always find what you want in the world if you have enough money. I don't believe the reports of men who've been paid off.

I pay men off to to say what I want. We, the
wealthy, know how the game is played. We sell
bullshit to the ignorant, trusting peasants and
they must buy what we sell because they have
no choice. Money is power—and that gives you
choices. One must know when and how to em-
ploy one's power and choices. A good soldier
knows when to eat well, but also when to then
become lean for the battle. Are you a good soldier, Juan?"

"*Sí*. The best," Anthony said without blinking,
hating Salazar the more the man talked.

"*Bueno!*" Roberto said, laughing, and then
bit into the massive shrimp he'd been waving
around. "Good men are replaceable, mercenaries
can always be found, a small army can always be
raised, but an excellent man with no fear is very
rare find indeed . . . just like it's hard to find a
good woman."

Roberto pushed back from the table and
wiped his mouth with a gold-toned silk napkin
and then threw it into his plate. The others at
the table stopped eating and waited.

"They stole from me my peace of mind today.
That is rarer still and there is no insurance pol-
icy to cover that. It was a message that my family could not be safe, my woman and one day
my children will not be safe . . . that is what you
are saying when you attack a man's home and
try to kidnap the woman he lives with—the one

who would one day be the mother of his children." Roberto pulled out his cell phone and sent a text message that no one could see and then put it back into his breast pocket. "So, Juan, since you are more than a good soldier—self-proclaimed as the best—you protect that which is very valuable . . . irreplaceable to me, *sí*? You guard that thing with your life and succeed where Bruno failed me, and you will be a very wealthy man."

The sound of feminine footfalls beside heavy boots twisted the shrimp in his gut as Roberto stood, making every man at the table get up. Sage entered the room with a dirty-faced, bloody guard who looked like he'd been in a firefight. Her white linen blouse was dirty and ripped, just like her pants. She hesitated when she saw him, and Roberto took note.

"It's all right. These men have checked out." Roberto opened his arms for her and she filled them, burying her face against his neck. He kissed the crown of her head fiercely with complete ownership and stroked her back. "You're safe now. I will make this all right."

For a moment, Anthony just stared at the food-laden table, unable to watch the ruse without emotion. But within seconds he'd recalibrated his expression. Any brief eye contact between them was processed by Salazar as her suspicion. His subsequently lowered gaze was seen as respect.

"Do you now see what I have at risk, Juan?" Roberto said to Anthony while caressing Sage's body. "This could have been taken from me today, but Rico has also earned himself a place at my table forever for this. I am rebuilding now from the ashes. You and Rico have separated yourselves out from average men. Therefore, you stay in this house until our business is finished and you travel with her as her escort at *all* times, *comprende*?"

Her hands trembled as she slipped off her dirty clothes and stepped into the shower. Hot water pummeled her body as she washed off the filth of battle. A pair of jeans, a T-shirt, panties, and tourist's sneakers had been hastily purchased for her on Bourbon Street by one of Roberto's men. Eye signals that bordered on telepathy let her know that as soon as Alvarez cleared the building, he'd inform Hank Wilson and the DEA team that she was alive, and they'd communicate that to DELTA.

But nothing in the world could have prepared her for coming face-to-face with Anthony in Salazar's dining room. It had felt like the bottom had dropped out of her stomach, the same feeling one experiences when an elevator descends too rapidly.

When the bathroom door opened, she jumped

and almost screamed. Roberto moved toward her and for a second she covered her breasts and pubic area with her hands.

"I cannot imagine what you've been through," he murmured, opening the glass shower door.

He waited for her to come to him and she eventually did, chewing her lip. But she shook her head, hugging herself; she couldn't submit to whatever he had on his mind. An earnest sob broke through her façade, and rather than infuriate him, it made him draw her out of the spray and into his arms.

"I just want to hold you," he said in a hoarse whisper. "To let you know that it would have cut my heart out if they'd gotten you today." He lifted her chin with a finger and then allowed his gaze to travel down her body. "Look at what they have done to my *tesoro* . . . the bruises . . . they've beaten you . . . tell me what else did they do!"

"They threw me in a trunk," she said, practically hiccup crying as the truth and the lies became muddled in her mind. Her tears seemed to suddenly wash all of that free. "They put a bag over my head, Roberto . . . tied me up with plastic handcuffs . . . then, then the car or van, I couldn't tell which, had an accident. It rolled over, there was smoke and shooting and—"

"And they didn't rape you," he said, releasing a long breath of relief briefly closing his eyes. "Or beat you with their fists . . . or splash battery acid on your gorgeous face."

He held her as she cried harder, stroking her wet, naked back, hips, and buttocks, never understanding why she was really sobbing..

"I'm so scared," she whispered thickly against his neck. "What's happening? Why are they doing this? Who are these terrible people?"

Inner knowing told her that this was the only way to avoid him. It was the same effective reverse logic that Cape fur seals used on great white sharks—one had to get close to the predator and swim alongside it long enough to break away fast so that the shark couldn't maneuver to turn around and bite you.

She knew that now more than ever before, she had to seem totally clueless about his enterprises and sufficiently freaked out to have a plausible reason for why she just couldn't flip a switch and make love to him on demand for a couple of days.

After a moment to collect his thoughts, his voice took on a frighteningly calm tone as he produced a knot of cash from his pocket and pressed it into her hand. "Those people are business competitors of mine who couldn't do business the honorable way, and decided to try to terrorize my household to make me comply. This is why I have always told you, stay with Bruno, *sí*?"

She nodded and wiped at her tears.

"When you do international business, sometimes things get very aggressive, Camille . . . this is why the wealthy have armored cars and security. This is why they keep the identities of their wives and children secret, and put locator chips in their bodies . . . because there are terrorists out there who would kidnap those they love. But that is under control now."

He drew back from her and held her face. "I want you to be my wife, Camille. The mother of my children. I was going to wait until I'd completed my business here in New Orleans before I asked for your hand . . . the jeweler is making your ring now as we speak. But after what just happened, I couldn't wait."

Kissing her gently, he enfolded her in his arms. Every nerve fiber within her screamed dissent as her conscience flogged her. She knew he was a monster, but he was also a man. She knew what he'd done and was still capable of doing was despicable, evil, horrific . . . but he was still a human being who bled red blood. Revenge never tasted so bitter. This betrayal would be something she'd have to live with for the rest of her life, and not because she feared for her life, but because she feared for her soul. Her grandmother was right—"vengeance is mine, sayeth the Lord."

When he broke the kiss, tears of remorse shimmered in her eyes. The lines had been blurred and some fragile, indefinable element of humanity had been breached in the battle of good guys versus bad guys. She touched his face knowing that she'd never be able to apologize to him for the transgression. That he was now processing her tears and touch incorrectly, leaving her helpless to set the record straight, made her weep for her enemy. Her family had died at his hand, but at least it had been quick. This man was being tortured to death, and she was many things, but she'd never thought herself cruel.

Wiping her silent tears, he smiled. "I'll accept that as a beautiful yes . . . So I want you to take this money and go with Juan while Rico gets stitched up, to get some decent clothes. But be quick and stay nearby, all right? Can you do that?"

"Okay," she said softly, touching the side of his face. "I didn't understand before, but I understand now. I'm sorry."

"*Bueno*," he murmured, and then took her mouth slowly.

Arturo Guzman made a tent with his fingers in front of his mouth and listened to the report his trusted inside man gave him. Sitting in the semi-darkness of his expansive office, he allowed the brandy-tipped, hand-rolled cigar to burn down in the ashtray, enjoying the aroma as tendrils of smoke wafted past his senses.

Roberto Salazar blew up his own house, yacht, and cars? Not possible. Sniper fire had not only taken out some of his men, but also had hit some of Salazar's men as well. And since when would a woman, a marrying kind of innocent, take out one of his hit men, jump into a Mercedes, and drive like a she-devil toward sure danger?

This stunk to high heaven, and he strained to understand the words coming across his desk in a thick Russian accent.

"Dimitri," he finally said, and then took up his cigar to puff it a bit before inhaling a long drag from it. "We have done business now for how many decades?"

The elegant, silver-haired gentlemen stared at each other with knowing smiles.

"Too long to count, Arturo. At least since the end of the cold war." Dimitri cut the end off his expensive cigar and lit it slowly with a gold-plated Zippo lighter from Guzman's desk.

"Does this sound like a young punk who is prepared for battle . . . or a third party?"

"Al Qaeda doesn't give a damn about Roberto's business ambitions, they merely want weapons to fight the Americans . . . which we will supply them, as the more stressed the Americans are, the more their economy suffers, the more of your product they demand. Very simple. Very efficient. The balance of power is maintained in the world. So I do not think they are your third party, and as weapons dealers and mercenaries, we have no advantage in aiding Roberto against you. He could not do this alone, I do not believe."

"You being involved never crossed my mind, Dimitri. That is not what I was signifying at all. And, I also agree. I cannot see Al Qaeda siding with a rogue drug dealer bent on profit alone and with no ideological link to their cause—not once they have extracted what they wanted from him—immediate cash for arms. But they are problematic, if they are now selling into my territories behind my back with very cheap product."

Dimitri chuckled. "Do not worry yourself. This pipeline to the US is unsustainable and they do not want to engage the stable cartel families in war. This will correct itself shortly, I assure you. We will help them understand there are better markets in Europe . . . by giving up a few of their cells for this transgression."

"Please encourage them quickly," Guzman muttered.

"As always." Dimitri released a long sigh and smiled at Guzman. "My friend, we old generals are familiar with the Afghans in a way that still eludes the young Americans. Remember how long Mother Russia was at war there before others came. The Taliban and Al Qaeda have absolutely no desire to pick a fight with you, and will fight for something intangible and worth more than money, according to their code—their version of honor."

When Guzman nodded, Dimitri took a long drag on his cigar and rolled it between his fat thumb and forefinger.

"Whether we agree that their cause is insane or not is immaterial, Arturo. What is interesting to me always is that they cannot be negotiated with as *individuals* for mere capital. But their chain of command understands that order within chaos is mandatory. That is what our young Roberto does not yet understand any more than the young government that fights them. The rebel Afghans are fighting something within their own society that has gone on for centuries. Understanding this requires cultural maturity that Roberto doesn't own."

"Impatience is what has led Roberto to break my heart," Guzman said, taking two quick angry puffs. "But you have a point. The people he did his deals with gain nothing by going to war with us here."

"No. That is why I would not think they set

these explosives. Their only aim in this relationship with Roberto is that they are very desperate for arms and have very disjointed infrastructure, which is what allowed them to actually patronize their competitor's arms business . . . yours, without knowing it. They knew they could not bring you excess product. Why would you give them cash for what you already produce? This makes no sense. So they look around and look around until they find someone who will buy what they have to sell in the large quantity they need to move."

"No one else would touch it. Anyone with that much cash is a competitor already linked into very old and very solid networks, Dimitri."

"Correct. This is how they wind up stealing a young, cocky customer of yours, Roberto, and then pay you back by purchasing your weapons— while young Roberto has no idea that you and I, as old friends, have long been in business together. It is a shame, actually. He has been in America too long . . . where a house divided cannot stand."

"What did you sell this Assad?" Arturo Guzman temporarily set down his cigar again and considered his old friend.

"It has been over a year since the American Nuclear Arms Treaty lapsed. A new spirit of dissention has fallen over the US. The new president has tried to get this *trust and verify* treaty ratified so that there can be inspections and enforcement . . . ahhh . . . but jealous opponents have become so factious that they think of only themselves and not their country as a whole. So, during this time of great debate and contentious behavior within the American government, the UN was secretly moving eleven tons of enriched uranium and three tons of plutonium, by rail in reinforced stainless steel casks, across eighteen hundred miles of open land in Kazakhstan—from the Aqtau nuclear site, very close to Chechnya across the Caspian Sea. That is enough to make eight hundred nuclear bombs . . . and all we needed was thirty-nine pounds of material to make one."

Guzman chuckled. "The old Americans were like us once, unified. Parties came together to fight a common cause. I have watched these debates. Obstructionists are more concerned with being individually right than ensuring the good of the whole. They throw the baby out with the bathwater. There is no compromise, but in a family, there must be compromises. This is what Roberto has done. He is thinking of himself, not the whole, and has won short-term gains . . . but this will not last."

"And we must embrace change. Not all change is bad." Dimitri chuckled. "We can now vote with our dollars in American elections. Ironic that their so-called Citizens United Supreme Court case allows us to *donate* as foreigners . . . so now, we can have their officials in our hip pockets to sway treaties as we like. We are virtually untouchable as power coalesces, my friend. Stay positive."

"*Sí,*" Guzman said, dragging on his cigar again. He stared into the air pensively. "I feel that Roberto has been infiltrated by another source."

Dimitri nodded. "This is high probability because he is young and impulsive and wants too much too fast. This allows for miscalculation. Whoever set those charges knew how to do it to eviscerate everything on that property."

"Military?"

"Possibly US military . . . since they are chasing Assad, I am sure. Or drug enforcement, perhaps CIA."

"Can your forces on the ground sweep the car the woman was driving? Roberto was like a son to me . . . I taught him much of what I know, and if he has fought so hard to have this woman returned to him, then I am pretty sure I know what he has done."

Dimitri laughed and poured himself more vodka from the crystal decanter that rested on the small oval table beside his leather chair. "Should I call Hector and allow him to be the hero?"

"I haven't decided."

"Aw . . . Arturo . . . throw the poor boy a bone for his troubles. He so wants to finally best his big brother."

"Hector is weak," Guzman said, crushing out his cigar. "Traitorous and weak, even if it did alert us to his brother's deal. I would have respected him more if he had either left Roberto and come to stay here with us, or gone with his brother and never tipped us off. But he took the coward's way out . . . being sneaky behind his own brother's back for a guarantee of *safety*, not even enough money to make the difference. So why should I reward that, my friend?"

"In Russia, we have an old saying . . . the enemy of my enemy is my friend." Dimitri took a long, thoughtful drag from his cigar and then studied the embers. "Wouldn't it be better to allow Hector this small victory of delivering very bad news to his brother . . . and as punishment for Roberto's betrayal, and to torture Roberto's soul for ever daring to betray you . . . you can then let Roberto know about his brother. Let each betrayer fall to their knees before Roberto's eyes and let him judge them harshly—as we know he will . . . and then remind him of his judgments when he must kneel before you and die. Yes?"

A slow, sinister smile took up the edge of Guzman's mouth as he lifted a brandy snifter to

Dimitri in salute. "The Russian way is not so very different from the Colombian way. We understand honor."

"Yes . . ." Dimitri murmured. "This is why we have been friends without incident for so long."

CHAPTER 12

Judging from the expression on Rico's face, he hadn't taken Roberto's decision to fill Bruno's post with a new man—Anthony—very well. Listening to Rico's detailed description of what happened at the compound, and how he'd saved Camille, apparently hadn't moved Roberto to change his mind.

By rights it should have been Rico's promotion, and Anthony said nothing as a house doctor on the payroll stitched up Rico's arm in the kitchen while Rico sent an angry glare out the window. After all, Rico had brought Roberto his prized possession, Camille. Then again, as far as the boss was concerned, a guy named Juan had just saved his life. Sad reality was, it was all a lie, all a game, and by morning there was a 90 percent chance they'd all be dead.

Anthony stood when Roberto entered the kitchen, but the old doctor never stopped sewing.

Roberto's immediate return relieved any fears he had about Sage being backed into a corner alone with him.

Meanwhile, Rico used the doctor's unceasing ministrations as an obvious excuse not to stand or look at his boss, and risk being shot again, fatally this time, for insubordination. Rico remained mute and just grimaced from the pain and only glanced at his injury. It was clear that he was pissed, but he was smart enough not to voice that fact. Only Hector seemed to silently acknowledge the slight, catching Rico's eye before looking away helplessly.

"Take her to the casino while I make new arrangements for our meeting tonight. What happened today changes many things. I have a lot to do . . . and she's shaken. Make her life normal. *Comprende?* There are plenty of upscale shops at Harrah's and we have men there, too, along with Assad's forces. I've informed them you will be there soon. With the crowds, it will be harder to target her at a twenty-six-floor, four-hundred-and-fifty-room hotel that also has its own security, than at a small boutique in the French Market. One RPG shell fired from a rooftop could take out a tiny, street-level store with only one way in and one way out, whereas a huge casino has multiple escape routes. Just like Jackson Square is wide open like the little shops around it; a sniper could be anywhere. You understand my point. I do not believe my enemy knows about my holdings here or about this particular property, but one can never be too sure."

Nodding, Anthony met Roberto's troubled gaze. "I understand. On my life, *nothing* will happen to her while she's under my guard."

"Good man," Roberto said, ignoring Rico's unspoken fury. He then looked at his brother. "*Vámanos.*"

Although dressed in a T-shirt and jeans, she felt naked without a gun. No purse, no lipstick, no sunglasses, no ID, she had nothing to help her create the façade of being Camille Rodriguez—Roberto Salazar's woman, now fiancée. It was the first time since she'd taken on the assignment that she felt so completely vulnerable. The affected airhead persona, the oblivious shopaholic, the vain beauty, all of it was an act carried off by makeup and high-end stage props.

But now, she was wearing what she normally wore in her real life. Her face was scrubbed clean of expensive makeup and she was about to go out into the world with the real man she wanted to be with. The terror of that acute exposure made her hands shake. And the moment she hit the bottom step of Roberto's French Quarter mansion, the wall between her real self and her undercover self came tumbling down.

"Ms. Rodriguez," Anthony said carefully, and

then glanced at Roberto across the grand marble foyer for confirmation. "I'll be your security detail. My car is in the courtyard, and I can take you over to Harrah's to shop and then bring you home."

Roberto nodded and went to her when she stopped and hugged herself at the bottom of the curved staircase. He cupped her cheek and spoke to her as though one would speak to a frightened child.

"Juan is all right, Corazón. As good as Bruno, if not better. Go get something nice to wear . . . some makeup and a beautiful dress for the Mardi Gras parties. Maybe we'll stay in New Orleans for a while or go on a little vacation and stay somewhere exotic while the house in Miami is rebuilt. When you come back, I'll have the doctor give you some Xanax to relax . . . and Maritsa can bring you a tray to your room, if you're hungry. Just tell her what you'd like to eat. In a day or so, we'll put all this behind us."

It was clear that he wanted to get her out of the house and away from him for a while. The tension in his face was unmistakable, just as his tight, jerky motions gave away the stress that was roiling beneath the false calm he presented.

Sage nodded and kissed him quickly, slipping out of Roberto's loose hold to go stand next to

Anthony. "Okay . . . I won't be long." She hated this, every last bit of it.

"*Bueno* . . ." Roberto replied, then turned away from her to head toward the library where his brother was waiting, and closed the huge pocket doors.

Two house guards who were packing heat followed them outside into the gated courtyard, casing it and Anthony's car before giving Anthony the signal that it was all right to bring her out and clear to enter his BMW. Sounds of New Orleans street jazz and hubbub filled her ears while she waited on their security check, wafting over the top of the iron gates in a humid cloud. The city had a daytime, happy persona that hid its dark side; her life mirrored the same duality.

Finally the guards slowly opened the gates so their car could pass. Her gaze roving, she noticed another man was on the roof surveying the ground below, which was teeming with tourist pedestrians.

Blocking both human and vehicle traffic so they could enter the narrow street, the guards gave them safe passage into the flow of humanity and then quietly disappeared inside the small citadel again. A block away and around the corner, Anthony broke the oppressive silence.

"This is an impound vehicle, we can talk."

"Has it been out of your sight?"

Anthony shook his head. "Visible from the dining room window out into the courtyard at all times. I kept the keys on me."

Sage released her breath. "Oh . . . man."

"Were you hurt?"

"No. Rico told you what happened?"

"I got it from three sources. Once when Alvarez called in the report, then from my DELTA unit, but it wasn't until Rico walked in the door with you that I knew you were alive and all right." He gripped the steering wheel tighter as they crept along in gridlocked traffic. "I can't tell you . . ."

She knew there was a part of the conversation they'd never be able to have, a part that he could never say—the part about how much he hated seeing Roberto physically claim her with hugs, kisses, and caresses.

"Yeah, well, you're a sight for sore eyes too, Captain," she said quietly, trying to lighten things between them with a snarky comment that fell flat due to her sad tone. Having failed her objective, she then wrapped her arms around herself and looked out the window.

"Back to Captain, after all of this?"

His dry comment made her smile, despite the insanity that was looming around them. "I need it for professional distance." She didn't dare look at him right away; he made her want to laugh and cry all at the same time.

"Roger that. Same reason I jammed my hands in my pockets when I saw that you were alive and had walked in under your own steam, instead of being bodily carried in."

She let out a long breath and finally looked at him. Running to him and hugging him hard was exactly what she'd wanted to do, too. But that would have been a death sentence for them both.

"Yeah," she murmured, wanting so badly to reach across the small space between them now and hold his hand but not daring to. No telling where eyes were. "So if you see me looking at the floor a lot . . ."

"Ditto," Anthony said as he navigated the car onto Canal Street. "But my hope is that dude is going to make his move soon. This bullshit needs to be over. Fucking mission accomplished already. The Colombians put added pressure on the situation and my worry is that Assad might just cut and run, now that he's been paid."

"True, but he's *still* at the casino," she said with emphasis. "What better place is there to wash money or do wire transfers or stash your excessive amounts of cash safely, if you have a man on the inside there?"

"Right."

"And . . . let's calm down and think about this thoroughly," she added, glancing at him and then back at the traffic. "If Assad is sticking around and has his own retinue of men still at the casino, it has to be to insure his weapons shipment. Not that I've met him, but he doesn't strike me as the kind of guy who would hand over cash based on a cell phone call coming out of Canada . . . unless . . ."

"Unless someone higher than him gives the okay." Anthony glanced at her and then back at the traffic. "An ironclad source."

"Exactly," Sage said and then placed a finger on her lips, thinking for a moment. "This could go right to the nerve center of a terror cell or a network of cells. If Assad did get such a call, then he could divvy up the cash and give it to physical couriers to travel in different directions. That way there isn't one big very obvious shipment, but several smaller ones. Also, his cash isn't in the same place as his weapons, in case anything went wrong . . . and if temporarily stopped, guys coming out of the casino with a large stash might not raise suspicions, if their phony paperwork looked legit."

"That and what if Assad hasn't been fully paid yet because Roberto is waiting for his distributors to do the buy?" Anthony glanced at Sage for a moment. "What if it was a half up-front, half when my distributors come to town kind of deal?"

"Damn . . ." Sage murmured. "That makes so much sense. It would have to be the only reason Assad is still here. Especially after all the chaos in Miami. Unless he had a real reason to stay, he should have been on the next thing smoking."

"My point exactly. And if that hunch proves valid, then we have an opportunity to ID anybody that's in his security retinue as a potential courier. We'll be able to follow them to the Canadian delivery and to anywhere else in the world they're taking the money." Anthony turned off Canal, heading toward the casino situated at the foot of it on Poydras Street. "This may be the last chance we have to talk like this for a while."

"I know," Sage said resigned. "But I'll only take like twenty minutes to grab a few items, get some makeup and toiletries, and then we can walk around the casino floor and see if we can spot Assad. I don't think I should be gone more than an hour."

"Agreed. We'll have a chance to reconvene in the car on the way back."

"Uh uh," she said, shaking her head. "Once this vehicle leaves your sight and is in valet custody, it could be bugged. You don't know who Roberto has called and you won't know what they've stashed in your car."

Anthony nodded as they pulled up into the valet station. "Sage Wagner, falling in love with you is making this soldier sloppy."

He got out of the vehicle and rounded it before she could answer or an eager valet could open her door, leaving her slack-jawed.

They walked into the brightly lit, French-styled, gold-and-ivory ornamental lobby that was accented with black-and-ivory diamond patterned marble floors. Pristine ferns, sumptuous centerpieces, and elaborate Victorian furnishings made them feel like they'd gone back in time to the antebellum south and had just stepped into the foyer of a huge plantation house. But she was numb to it all.

Wresting back her focus, Sage headed to the concierge's desk to get her bearings after the bomb Anthony had just dropped on her and to inquire about the shops. Thankfully the shopping pavilion was on the other side of the casino floor, which gave them a reasonable excuse for passing through it.

Anthony caught her sidelong glance. They were on the same page. She thanked the ebullient hotel staffer and withdrew with Anthony to do a reconnaissance around the high roller sections of the floor.

"Poker or baccarat?" she said in a low murmur. "Place your bets."

"My money's on baccarat," Anthony said, ushering her through the crowd by her elbow, but keeping a very respectable distance, lest they be seen by one of Salazar's roving patrols. "More of a foreigner's game."

She allowed a half smile to capture her face. "You'll owe me dinner in Chicago if you're right."

"Okay," he said.

"You weren't processing what I said." She chuckled softly and kept walking.

"Heeey . . . wait a minute."

"Yeah." She laughed harder, but not too hard. "Generally if you win a bet, you get to set the terms."

"Maybe I was subconsciously setting the terms. Sounds like winner takes all to me."

"Touché," she said calmly, not looking at him but smiling as they passed the baccarat salons. "And it's dinner in Chicago."

She watched Anthony make eye contact with Assad, who nodded at him briefly like a trusted member of the group. Three men were with him.

"Wanna fill me in?" she said as they stepped into the main shopping thoroughfare off the casino floor.

"Haneef Massoud, Daoud El-Sayed, and Nazir Salahuddin. Right up in the top ten most-wanted by Intelligence along with Assad. Four of a kind beats a full house every time. We get all four, plus whoever is gonna make that Canada call, and it's a damned royal flush. They weren't here when this began."

"I take it that this means your man is waiting for the second half of his payment."

"Absolutely," Anthony said in a murmur as she stopped in front of a designer shop. "Ten minutes in here, tops."

"I know. We have to get back . . . and more importantly, we've gotta get to a secure phone."

Anthony watched Sage slip into a ritzy shop and stood guard just outside. He could see her through the glistening plate glass window, and there really wasn't anywhere for her to go or for an attacker to slip in without him seeing the abduction.

This was the hard part. The waiting while knowing there were a thousand things he needed to do and communicate but couldn't without potentially blowing their covers.

Yet in the midst of the madness, his nerves frayed and close to popping, he'd further compromised their psyches by telling her something so deep, ill-timed, and intimate that he wanted to kick his own ass. The truth had simply leapt out of his mouth as though he'd been water-boarded!

He had to get a grip, had to focus on Assad now that his full inner circle was here in the States with him. That could lead to Aalam Bashir, someone they'd been hunting for since 2001.

Ways to get word to his unit clawed at his mind, until he saw Agent Alvarez casually strolling toward him.

"Hombre, whassup?" Alvarez said, grabbing Anthony's hand and pulling him into a familiar urban homeboy embrace.

"Need a word, man."

"I know you do," Alvarez said, giving the casino cameras his back and looking through the
window at Sage. He spoke barely moving his
lips and kept his voice low. "We've got eyes, too,
watching everything coming in and out of the
compound in the Quarter. Saw your Beemer
leave with our girl in it. Hallelujah. Plus, trucks
have been on the move from the docks since
this afternoon—that's the word. Cleaned out the
shipping containers on the freighter. All the ones
we're worried about went to Key West Construction warehouses. It's cool for me to be here
playing a little blackjack and killin' time with
the other distributors, feel me? "

"Yeah, man, I feel you," Anthony said, keeping an eye on Sage and then glancing at Alvarez.
"I've got three names that I need you to get to
my unit—Haneef Massoud, Daoud El-Sayed, and
Nazir Salahuddin. If you can't remember, tell my
unit, the big three are with the king and playing
baccarat. Check lines of credit coming out of this
joint and any wire transfers headed to Canada."

"Done," Alvarez muttered. "You ready for tonight?"

"As ready as I can be."

"We saw you come into the valet bay. Got
your car covered. Look under the seat for some
hit. Give it to her. You'll find two encrypted cells

and a couple of clips in the glove compartment. It's down to the wire now, man. Anything can pop off at any time."

"Good looking out."

"*De nada.*" Alvarez looked through the glass and then at Anthony full-on. "How's our girl?"

"As well as can be expected, under the circumstances . . . a little banged up but thankfully not brutalized."

Alvarez nodded and then put out his fist for Anthony to pound it. "Then she's doing real good, bro. Especially under the circumstances."

CHAPTER 13

She saw Agent Alvarez talking to Anthony
through the plate glass of the store window and
hurried. But she waited until the two men parted
before she actually exited the shop. Anthony collected her at the door and she kept her expression casual as they walked and she found a place
that sold makeup, perfumes, and expensive toiletries.

"Good news?"

"Never better," he said and then glanced
around. "You've got phone and heat in the car.
We'll talk there. It's covered."

She nodded, handed Anthony her bags, and
stepped into the store.

Moving as though on a timed game show, she
was in and out of the small, glitzy emporium in
a flash. From this point on, she and Anthony
were pure motion, heading back to the car that

would guarantee them a few moments of strained privacy. Once inside it, she began digging into one of the larger bags for a purse she'd bought, yanking off the tags, and simultaneously feeling under the seat for the promise of salvation.

Her hands touched familiar steel and she nearly gasped in relief. But never missing a beat she leaned forward and discreetly stashed it in her large, metallic purse, then extracted the clips from the glove compartment, discreetly handed Anthony two, hid two in her handbag, and looked at both cell phones. Written in water soluble marker on a piece of cellophane tape on each phone were the cell phone numbers. She repeated both to Anthony until he nodded and could repeat them back to her, then she licked her thumb and erased the numbers, wiping the light blue ink on her dark jeans.

"Feel better?" he asked in a low, serious rumble.

"Never better . . . now."

"Ditto."

"You know I may have to leave you in there tonight," Anthony said.

"I know that. Roberto will never have me anywhere near that meeting." She glanced over at Anthony. "So far I've been pretty lucky . . . haven't used up all my nine lives yet."

"I'm just worried that you're dancing on number nine, Sage—"

"Camille," she corrected gently. "You can't

worry about that when you go in there. You more than anybody knows what can happen if a soldier loses focus. I need you to come back for me." Her voice fractured as it dropped to a harsh whisper. "Promise me."

"You only have to ask me that once, baby."

She nodded and stared out the window.

There were no logistics to discuss, nothing else to say . . . nothing that was safe. She'd fallen in love with a soldier and it had happened so fast, so furiously, in the heat of combat that, there was no explanation for it. And it was the last thing either of them needed right now yet also everything they'd always needed. It was ill-timed, inconvenient, and totally insane. Anthony's voice made her insides flutter as he spoke in low, commanding bursts to his unit over the encrypted cell phone, getting intel on the movement of the contraband from the docks. Pedestrians were a blur as Roberto's compound came into view.

"I heard you loud and clear, Captain," she said as the gates opened. She waited for him to nod. "Ditto. Remember that."

He got out of the vehicle without a word and rounded it, opening the door for her, both of them well aware that unseen eyes were observing them. She walked ahead of him with her head held high, resigned to whatever fate had in store for them.

Thankfully, Roberto didn't greet her at the back of the house. Only guards were there with Maritsa.

"You must eat, Señorita," the older woman urged quietly, and then produced a small vial of Xanax. "This will help."

"Just some toast and a bottled water so this settles on my stomach, all right?" Sage replied, accepting her bags from Anthony. There was no way in the world she was ingesting anything from the wrong side this close to a sting, especially when it was clear that Roberto wanted her to stay quiet and oblivious to all that was happening around her. "*Gracias.*"

"*De nada,*" he said quietly, and then left her side.

"Boss is in the library," one of the guards informed Anthony on his way out of the kitchen.

She stared after Anthony for a moment and then went upstairs via the back staircase, nerves filleting by the second. As soon as she got in her room she ripped into her bags, changing so that she'd be ready for any eventuality, ready to hit the streets packing.

Black leather pants, red off-the-shoulder sweater, low-heel boots to make kicking ass and running practical—she changed down to the drawers and a push-up bra for dramatic effect and in order to pass inspection.

As Sage was beating her face with powder and

applying mascara, Maritsa brought up a tray with toast and water. Thanking the older woman and accepting the tray, Sage closed the door on her, not allowing Maritsa to witness her take the meds. Those were going down the sink. Then there was nothing to do but wait.

He walked into the library and found Roberto there with Hector and Rico.

"Thank you for keeping an eye on Camille," Roberto said, pouring a Scotch. "Tonight, I need fast hands at my side, in case we have another problem like we had earlier."

Anthony nodded, measuring Rico's fury and something about Hector that he couldn't figure out yet.

"So since Rico is wounded and has already earned a purple heart, I'm asking him to stay here with house guards to make sure my prized possession isn't harmed. You will go over with the advance guards and make sure that the warehouse is clear. Then you will call me, and I will then have Hector inform the other four distributors that it is clear to proceed. Do you have a problem with walking point?"

"None at all."

"*Bueno* . . . because, after all, my mentor once told me that a man he respected once said, 'trust but verify.' I trust you, Juan . . . but I must verify that this afternoon wasn't just a fluke or lucky reflexes. Asking a man to walk point in a very dangerous deal is a way to verify."

"Understood."

Roberto turned to Rico. "Camille is to be my wife . . . the future mother of my children. If there is a breach in this compound, you die making sure she lives or die by my hand if she doesn't."

"*Sí*, Jefe," Rico said, but with an angry sneer, glancing at his wounded arm. "You have verified me and I haven't failed you."

Roberto nodded and lifted a glass toward Rico. "Don't be jealous of Juan. It is an emotion that can divide brothers. Do I not treat you as a brother, and reward you well?"

"*Sí*, Roberto," Rico mumbled, looking away.

"In this time of rebuilding, we cannot have a division between brothers. No one is putting Juan over you—there are different times for different skills."

Rico nodded and looked up at Juan.

"Shake," Roberto commanded. "One day in a firefight you may have to have each other's backs."

To ease the tension, Anthony stepped forward first and extended his hand. Rico grudgingly accepted it. Roberto smiled and knocked back his drink, although Hector remained oddly detached and passive.

"*Bueno!*" Roberto said, and then dismissed Anthony and Rico with a wave of his hand.

"Before we leave, can I speak to you, brother?" Hector asked quietly.

Anthony kept walking, not liking the sound of Hector's request. There was something frightened and too skittish about it when addressing his blood brother. But he couldn't linger to investigate it. Two burly guards now flanked him and were escorting him to the cars as Rico went to join the others in the kitchen.

Hector poured a drink with shaking hands and took a timid sip from it. Roberto barely noticed his brother's birdlike motions as he found his nine-millimeter in the study's mahogany desk drawer and checked the clip in it.

"After tonight, the little setback we experienced earlier will be forgotten and we will be very rich men." Roberto stared at his brother now. "I've invested five million, cash, and my distributors will each bring a million—combined that makes ten million dollars' worth of product this pure, that will soon net ten and a half times that in street value once it's flipped. A hundred and fifty million dollars. I don't even have to use my profit to replace whatever got damaged or destroyed today. Insurance pays for that because I'm a law-abiding citizen."

He laughed and lifted his glass to Hector. "Then the five I invested comes right back to me, when Assad completes his weapons deal."

Leaning into his brother, Roberto pressed his point. "I have actually invested *nothing,* and will come away with seventy-five million dollars . . . *for nada.* Do you understand what a coup that is? That will put me firmly into the billionaire's club before I am forty, and I have a steady, eager supplier in Assad."

"This would have only been a coup if Guzman hadn't found out," Hector said quietly, stepping away from Roberto. "Maybe . . . maybe if you tell him you did this for him, to bring this new alliance into the family, he'll forgive you or understand?"

"What . . ." Roberto whispered in a lethal murmur. "Are you loco, Hector?"

"No," he said, lifting his chin. "But I think sometimes your ambition drives you too far. What happened today convinced me. Guzman will not stop until he wipes you off the face of the map . . . and no amount of money will ever give you peace if he feels he's been betrayed. Do not go to this meeting. I have a bad feeling. Call him," Hector pleaded. "Talk to him. He loves you like a son, Roberto!"

"Do you hear yourself, Hector?" Roberto said, shaking his head. "You sound so weak and so insane." He set down his drink and just looked at the gun on his desk. "Go to Guzman, crawl on my knees, and apologize . . . and suck his dick that he might allow me back into the fold after what I have done."

"*Sí,*" Hector whispered.

"You would actually tell your brother—me—to suck a man's dick to keep from dying!"

"No . . . I'm just asking you to think, Roberto! You may be worth two or three billion; he is worth ten times that, maybe a hundred. How can you fight that or his network? Today, he showed you what he could do!"

"No!" Roberto shouted, rounding the desk to stand in Hector's face. Grabbing his brother by the suit jacket lapels, he shoved him. "Today I showed him!" he added, slapping his chest. "I showed that old man that I am not afraid, that I am a businessman who is ready to fly on his own, if not moved up quickly enough! Gone are the old days. This is a new world. And I showed Arturo that I am not afraid!"

"I don't want to die and don't want to see my brother dead," Hector said through unshed tears. He swallowed hard and straightened his rumpled jacket.

"Then you are clearly in the wrong business." Roberto moved back to his desk and holstered his weapon. "What happened to you? We used to run the corners together . . . and now I don't know who you are."

"We were poor. Had nothing to lose, then."

"So prosperity has made you soft, like Bruno and the others?"

"No," Hector said, lifting his chin. "I just got a chance to have my belly filled and everything I've ever wanted. That was enough for me. I didn't need more."

Roberto nodded and considered his brother with sad eyes. "I know. You never needed more. That is the difference between you and me." He released a long sigh. "You stay here like a woman with my Camille and Rico will protect you both."

She heard loud voices, then angry male footsteps rushing up the stairs. Sage braced herself, but no one came barreling into her bedroom. A door down the far end of the hallway slammed. Then as she went to the window, lying back in the shadows of it, she saw Roberto leaving with several armed guards.

It was imperative to know who was still in the house. Taking the toast off the tray, she broke it up into small pieces and then flushed the toilet. After a beat, she sucked in a deep breath and went into the main section of the master bedroom, gathered up the small silver tray, and slipped into the hallway.

Walking as silently as possible, she hurried in the direction that she'd heard the door slam, and then slowed her steps as she heard Hector's voice.

His words were partially muffled, but the little that she did make out made her eyes widen. Hector's panic-laden voice had become shrill, resonating at a pitch that allowed her to hear every third word. The moment he hung up the call, she quickly tiptoed to the back staircase and walked down it to the kitchen, giving Rico and Maritsa a start.

"*Señorita!*" Maritsa exclaimed. "*Madre de Dios.*" The older woman closed her eyes and swept toward Sage to take her tray. "You scared the life out of me. *Por favor,* you should be resting."

"Things are bad here in the house, Camille," Rico said in a cautious tone. "You need to announce yourself . . . the guys' nerves are sprung and the last thing we need is for them to accidentally hurt you."

"I'm so sorry," she said, dragging her fingers through her hair. "I heard yelling, couldn't tell who was shouting or what was being said . . . and then a door slammed. I got scared."

Rico glanced at another bodyguard who was standing by the door before speaking. "Just Hector and Roberto having a brother-to-brother disagreement, as always. Nothing to worry about."

Sage nodded. "Okay . . . I guess I'm still a little jumpy after everything. I think I'll take another pill."

"Don't worry. We all understand . . . you've been through a lot." Rico let out a hard breath. "We're all gonna be like that for a while."

Sage hugged herself. "I know this sounds silly, but . . . how many people are in the house?"

"Doesn't sound silly at all," the guard at the door muttered.

Rico nodded. "There's ten of us right now. Seven guards including me, you, Hector, and Maritsa—who will be going home for the day in a little while. So don't worry. You're safe."

Rico's voice didn't sound sure, apparently not even to Maritsa.

"If you don't mind, Señor . . . may I leave now?" Maritsa said, taking off her apron. "All of this shouting and guards is making me *nervioso*. I'm sorry," she added, making the sign of the crucifix over her chest. "I must go. Give my apologies to Señor Salazar for having to leave early."

Sage stood behind Maritsa with Rico and the guard by the kitchen door as the older woman fetched her big black pocketbook and hurried out of the door. She couldn't blame the woman and was glad she was gone—at least this way there were no civilians in the house for whatever might go down here.

CHAPTER 14

Construction yard gravel bit into his tires as his vehicle left the main warehouse road. Every bump and crunch under his wheels felt like shrapnel assaulting his nervous system. Anthony kept his eyes sweeping. A black Escalade and two black Beemers were his escort, filled with men as wary as he was. He had to trust that his men were in position, but where were the Colombians?

After several passes through the dead truck yard, the driver of the black Escalade rolled up beside Anthony's vehicle and lowered his window.

"All ten trucks are at the loading docks. You go in first and make sure the drivers check out." He smiled in a lopsided sneer. "If you walk back out, we'll go in and sweep the warehouse with you."

Anthony nodded, checked the clip in his nine-millimeter, and rolled up to the loading dock knowing all eyes were on him. He'd either get a bullet in his back from Roberto's suspicious men or several in the chest from drivers who didn't know him—or Colombians who assumed he was a betrayer, which he was by all counts.

He stepped through the darkened loading dock door and ten armed drivers with several shotgun riders nodded at him as he walked across the floor.

"Roberto's security team needs to sweep the building before the meeting," he called out to the most menacing driver.

A pair of dark eyes considered him and then nodded. Anthony turned on his heel, straining to hear the slightest movement or a hammer click, and walked back out into the late afternoon sunlight. Then he motioned to the black Escalade waiting in the distance.

"Vamanos!"

Hours had gone by, and she was bouncing off the wall. From her high window she could see Mardi Gras revelers clogging the streets and the sound of New Orleans jazz thrummed outside the windows. The city had its own pulse that could practically be felt through the floorboards.

But being trapped in the bedroom was, for all intents and purposes, like being on a stakeout. Boring. Long. Tiresome. But necessary.

As far as the men in the house knew, she'd

taken a Xanax and was out cold. Trying to get a call off would be foolhardy, in case there was a hidden camera or mic. She'd even body-blocked washing the pill down the sink and faked taking it with her water. Then she had taken a few fake bites of toast, inconspicuously spit them in her hand, and finally washed her hands so the bread would melt into the pipes unseen. Although she hadn't eaten all day, the last thing she could stomach was food, not when stress nausea had replaced hunger.

So she watched Mardi Gras from the window, her gaze sweeping the street for any incursion, her gun only an arm's length away in her purse on the nightstand. But her mind was a million miles away.

"Camille!"

Hector's angry voice shattered the calm. Something was wrong. His tone prepared her for battle as she dashed into the hallway with her weapon and headed for the back stairs.

Several footfalls stampeded up the main staircase, and she could hear a man rushing up the back steps.

"*Puta Negro!* You fucking whore!"

Hector hit the hallway landing at the same time Rico burst through the top hallway door. Brandishing his cell phone, Hector raised a Beretta and squeezed hard, Rico pushed Sage out of the way yelling.

"What the fu—"

The bullet hit Rico square in the chest. Blood splatter stained the back stairs hall door before his body dropped to the hardwood floor with a loud thud. Men yelled in the near distance just behind Hector. Sage fired instantly, blowing Hector back into the arms of the men who'd just reached the landing. Then she screamed for dramatic effect. She'd meant to hit his arm, that part was on purpose. But he lunged at her at the last moment, causing her to nail him in the right side of his chest—now in the chaos, him still living might create a diversion that could save her life. Taking him into custody alive had been the plan. DEA could descend on him once he was in a hospital. But he wouldn't last long with that much blood loss. Shit!

Weapon lowered, she spoke in a high-pitched panic to the men who'd surrounded the boss's brother. Her life depended on keeping the confusion swirling. "He tried to kill me and Rico!"

"What the fuck happened?" a guard shouted, afraid to shoot her and find out he'd been wrong, clearly not knowing what to do.

"He shot Rico!" she screamed, crumpling against the wall to maintain her cover and told the truth: It was self-defense. "He came up shouting and waving a gun. Then he pointed it at me."

Nervous guards split up, two standing over

Rico's dead body, knowing that it was hopeless, while four others held Hector.

"C'mon, man . . . c'mon, man. We gonna get Doc to get you straight. Hang in there," a blood-ied guard said, trying to stop the torrent of blood gushing from Hector's chest.

"No, man—it's fucking Mardi Gras!" another panicked guard shouted. "We've gotta get him to a hospital now, homes. He'll bleed out wait-ing on Doc or an ambulance."

"Okay, okay, get the car," the one holding Hector said as another guard tried to staunch the bleeding with his jacket. "Oh, man, why you gotta get loco on us now while Roberto ain't here. What the fuck, man?"

Hector's mouth began moving even as his eyes rolled back. It was evident that he was trying to tell them something, but the overwrought guards were more focused on trying to save his life.

"Do something, bitch! Get a towel or some-thing!" the man working on the wound yelled.

Blocked from the front hallway stairs by the men gathered around Hector, and with her room and the general bathroom at the other end of the hall beyond their frenetic chaos, she passed Ri-co's body and fled down the back stairs to the kitchen to supposedly fetch towels.

She never stopped running. Out the back door, into the courtyard holding a gun, she quickly maneuvered the gate latch and cracked the heavy metal barrier open, and then slipped through it. Looking back once, she saw one of Roberto's men at the now open bedroom window, but at least she had a head start on them.

During Mardi Gras, it was definitely faster running through the French Quarter than trying to navigate traffic. The narrow streets were clogged with very happy, very inebriated tourists, and the main thoroughfares were clogged with floats, bands, and marchers of all stripes. In that regard, it was a great place to get lost in and the din of the crowd was even enough to drown out the occasional gunshot—something that would be attributed to the party and not a homicide tonight, which—depending on who was shooting—was either a very good thing or a very bad thing.

Stashing her weapon beneath her blouse in the back waistband of her pants, she shoved past sweaty painted bodies, jumping a float procession, to head away from the river and the Bourbon Street and Canal Street mayhem. Her cell was back at the house, abandoned with her purse. She had to get to a hotel desk, a police station, somewhere she could commandeer a phone and find quick cover from the two men she was sure had come out on foot to follow her.

Ducking into an alley, she quickly caught her breath. Four would stay with the fallen—two riding in the front seat as driver and man riding shotgun, two in the back to carry Hector and hold him up. That was the safest bet to ensure Roberto didn't shoot them for allowing his brother to bleed to death on the house floor. But two had to recover her to either save her from sure danger in the streets with Colombians lurking nearby, or to bring her to justice for shooting his brother . . . and for whatever crimes Hector had found out she'd committed against the family.

Pushing away from the wall, she headed back out into the street and ran toward the Hotel Monteleone. DEA had to have seen her leave the house on foot followed by two or more gunmen. As she rounded the corner, an agent wearing a Kevlar vest came out of the shadows and turned to fire at a pursuer, but a rooftop sniper's bullet slammed into his vest, sending the agent sprawling. Sage flattened herself against the wall for a second to take dead aim at the man running toward her, and jumped back as his head exploded several feet from her.

Grabbing the fallen agent by the vest, she dragged him into the dark shadows of an alley and felt for his vitals. He was alive, Kevlar had saved him, but somebody didn't mean for him to make it.

Quickly finding his radio, she opened a channel and looked at the streets from the shadows.

"Man down! Man down, hit in vest, still breathing—in the alley on Iberville between Burgundy and Dauphine. We've got a sniper. Must be Colombian, because they took out one of Salazar's men. I've been made. Out!"

She loosened the man's vest and made sure he could breathe, and took a defensive position behind a Dumpster in the narrow alley to protect the fallen. If she left him, they'd put a bullet in his head. But a shadow at the far end of the alley didn't call out to her that he was DEA or raise a weapon when the unidentified caught a glimpse of her. Instead of barreling forward, he disappeared.

Sage looked up and moved along the wall with her weapon cocked. They might be jumping rooftops to fire down on her from a strategic position or rounding the building to do a quick takedown. She headed out into the street, running now, forced to leave the fallen man. When she looked over her shoulder she saw agents converging on the alley. That could have been what spooked the shooter. A man's foot splattered with blood was barely noticeable as she passed it—but he had on expensive Italian leathers. Had to be one of Roberto's. His two security henchmen who had been chasing her were history. So were whatever secrets they carried. The Monteleone was only a couple of blocks away.

Something stabbed into her neck. She whirled

on the sensation, her elbow connecting with facial cartilage, as she brought her knee up to a groin and stomped down hard on a kneecap that shattered. Stumbling backward, she yanked the needle out of her neck and grabbed onto a street lamppost. New Orleans was loud and hot and chaotic and confusing and blurry . . . but someone caught her before she hit the ground.

Agent Alvarez, posing as Rene Santiago, stood beside him, and Anthony kept his eyes forward as Roberto walked along the open truck bays. He'd been introduced to Dominic Reyes, Sammy Garza, and Alfonzo Gutierrez, and he was filling in for Miguel Estevez, who'd been taken into police custody to make room for his entry at the table.

Interestingly enough, Anthony noted, Assad and his men were also here. At this juncture, they were probably only concerned with getting their money, which was to be provided by Alvarez and the four other distributors.

The product checked out and the trucks were loaded. Each distributor had a large black case with a million dollars in it that they slid across the floor to Assad and his three men. Assad picked up two cases and each of his men took one.

"At the casino, we will wait for the word from Aalam Bashir to transfer funds to your man, Charles Wallace . . . once our weapons are in place." Assad calmly turned and walked away, each man getting into a nondescript rental car and driving off.

"You have just made a very wise choice to become wealthy men," Roberto said, smiling. "Each one of these trucks will take a different route with armed guards along the route to your legitimate warehouses, and then in much smaller weight via vans to your processing plants. The hard part is done. Now you just have to sell the goddamned product!"

Laughter rang out in the warehouse. A guard handed Roberto a bottle of chilled Cristal, and then a forklift rolled forward with cases of the bubbly. Guards worked quickly to break open cases and began handing out cold champagne to the distributors and their men.

"A toast," Roberto said, popping his cork. "To being wealthy motherfuckers and Mardi Gras!"

More laughter rang out as champagne head splashed on the ground and bottles belched open. But Anthony and Alvarez watched as Roberto took a call, his expression darkened, and the bottle he'd been holding slid from his grip to shatter on the cement floor. Silence instantly eclipsed all merrymaking. Roberto held up his hand to keep guards from firing as a car sped up, careening into the driveway, and a bloody, gasping guard jumped out of the BMW.

"She shot Hector! Rico is dead!" he shouted, breathing hard. "Two of our men went after her, Mario and Manuel, and they're now dead in the street! DEA is all over this. Hector was trying to warn us! This was on his phone, Roberto!"

The distraught guard tossed Roberto the cell phone and he stood motionless, playing back the shaky video. From Anthony's vantage point, the images were damning. Sage was in the red Mercedes in hot pursuit of the Colombians who had hit Bruno and then fired on her team. Something in the dashboard or mirror of the vehicle had been recording. In the heat of battle, she'd called in to DEA for reinforcement. She did not look like a distraught fiancée or an innocent. She looked like a cop, a badge, law enforcement, and from the look on Roberto's face, if he found her first, she wouldn't live long to explain.

"What's this mean, Roberto?" Alfonzo Gutierrez called out. "We need to move this shit pronto, hombre, if you got a fucking leak. Your woman is DEA? Is that who fucked up a hundred and fifty mil? You stupid—"

Roberto drew on Gutierrez like lightning, but multiple gun clicks from his security and Roberto's created a temporary standoff.

"Move the trucks and get my product out of here," another distributor shouted.

The armed driver teams nodded and headed for their trucks. Then all hell broke loose.

CHAPTER 15

Machine-gun fire strafed the trucks' cabins, shattering windows and instantly killing the drivers. Distributors scattered, shooting out of the truck bays at the loading dock and taking cover, not sure who the enemy was or where they were coming from. Mercenary commandos stormed the building and grabbed a fleeing Roberto, but they didn't execute him. It wasn't DELTA, it wasn't DEA—that much Anthony knew for sure. He hadn't given the order, nor had Alvarez, but once the shooting started, his unit and Alvarez's team would drop the hammer.

From Anthony's vantage point, flattened on the ground beneath a partially raised pallet, he could see that they'd forced Roberto into a van. There was only one group in the equation that had enough reason to do this: Guzman's men.

Agent Alvarez covered him as he called in the

van tags, yelling over the din. They had to follow the van and not apprehend it.

"Follow the van, tags Victor, Bravo, Charlie, Alpha three eight one five!"

"Get out of there, Captain!"

A spray of machine-gun shells opened up cement bags and splintered building supplies over their heads. Grabbing Alvarez by the back of his suit, Anthony yanked him to safety, yelling as they ran, "Go, go, go, go!"

The moment they rounded the back of the building, Anthony gave the order, "Send in Apaches hot!" Then he began running with Alvarez into the network of buildings.

The concussion from the blast threw them forward on their faces. In the distance, the sound of helicopter blades beat a deadly tempo in the air. Both men covered their heads as the intense heat from two hundred yards away washed over their skins. But there was no time for a full recovery.

Davis pulled Alvarez to his feet and they ran deeper into the warehouses, coming out on the other side of a preplanned escape route building where Captain Davis's unit was waiting.

"Nothing's coming out of that warehouse alive, not even cockroaches, sir. All product trucks are destroyed."

"Good work, Lieutenant Hayes. This is Special Agent Michael Alvarez. Our man on the inside."

"You guys don't bullshit with the firepower," Alvarez said, looking around the camouflaged team and then at the billowing inferno behind them. "Our evidence just went up in smoke, but I guess that's all right, because other than Roberto Salazar, you just wiped out his inner circle. Hector Salazar may be hanging by a thread in a hospital or dead by now."

"What's the word on Special Agent Sage Wagner?" Anthony's nerves stretched and popped as he looked at Alvarez and then his men.

"I cannot confirm," Lieutenant Hayes said, glancing at Lieutenant Butcher. "Our post was here, at the docks, and trailing Assad at the casino. DEA had the Salazar compound, where Special Agent Wagner was located."

Anthony felt the muscle in his jaw pulse as Alvarez called in to his team. While waiting, he kept drilling his men for critical mission information.

"The docks are secure?"

"Affirmative, Captain," Lieutenant Hayes said quickly. "The freighter was detained, two Kazakhstan nationals and three Colombians were taken into custody, along with a shipment of rocket-propelled grenade launchers, crates of AK-47s, Kevlar vests, C4—we have a full inventory report of what we confiscated. When we opened up the outer crates, all of it had stamps on it from Fort Shevchenko."

"Assad?"

Lieutenant Butcher stepped up. "Our units headed them off at the main highway, sir. They're in our custody and the money is, too."

"Hold them and keep the wire transfer lines open at the casino. Before you do anything, I want to talk to Intelligence about this shipment at the docks. What you confiscated does sound like five or even ten million dollars' worth of equipment. Something bigger is coming into Canada, either that or something more expensive."

"We lost her," Alvarez suddenly announced.

Anthony spun on Alvarez and gripped him by his lapels. "What do you mean you lost her?"

Alvarez placed an easy palm on Anthony's chest, forcing him to release his hold on his jacket, while the bewildered men in his unit cast confused glances between them. Anthony ran his palms down his face.

"Talk to me, Mike," Anthony said, beginning to pace.

"Something blew up at the house. You and I both saw from the video on Hector's phone that her cover was blown. Our agents tailed her out into the Mardi Gras celebrations in the streets. Two guards from the house were on her; we got one and an unknown shooter got the other one. We think it was Colombians. Same mercenaries that strafed the truck bays and took Roberto just now. They hit one of our agents, who was thankfully wearing a vest . . . Wagner stayed with him and called in man down, but was forced from her position by multiple shooters in hot pursuit. We found her Glock nine-millimeter about two blocks from the Hotel Monteleone, where she must have been going for cover. That was the last known location when our street team lost her."

"Put a bird up—pull out one of the portables from a truck, Lieutenant."

"But, sir, our mission is—"

"Do it now!" Anthony shouted. "I'm aware of our mission. Special Agent Wagner has insight to the Canada connection," he added, embellishing the scenario to get his men to move.

Boots hit the ground as men peeled out of Jeeps to head toward a parked eighteen-wheeler that contained a concealed chopper. Lieutenant Butcher threw Anthony a vest, which he caught with one hand, then tossed back.

"I'm going in light, just need artillery, grenades, and a sniper rifle."

His men nodded.

"We're going to get her back," Alvarez said. "Wherever they took Roberto is when you'll find her. It's the Colombian way to show a man his sins before executing him . . . at least at that level. They know his fiancée was DEA now. That's gonna call for a brief review before they torture him."

Anthony looked at Agent Alvarez hard.

"Yes . . . and how do you rub a man's nose in his own stupidity—you torture what he loved if front of him. Even after the betrayal, you desecrate it while he watches helplessly."

She woke up tied to a chair in an abandoned building. Mosquitoes feasted on her through the open windows. Moonlight showed nothing around the small building but junglelike flora. A tree actually grew up from under the house, through the floor, and up and out of the roof. Something skittered by in the corner. The stench of mold and mildew filled her nostrils. Feral animals made the tall grass rustle. Wild pigs and river rats, scrawny dogs and pathetic cats made their home here. As the haze left her mind, the lower Ninth Ward snapped into focus. Like a war-torn land, there were blocks and blocks of uninhabited houses. Her screams would go unheard and her body was unlikely to be found for days . . . months . . . years . . . if at all, once the animals had their way.

Struggling against her bindings, she tried to no avail to break off the wood or use it to saw against the ties. But all she managed to do was make the bindings cut deeper into her wrists.

The sound of a vehicle approaching, first one then another, stilled her. A door opened and she could tell it was a van of some sort because of the way the metal made a sliding sound before it slammed shut again. Multiple footfalls hit rotten wood steps, and the rickety door busted off its hinges. Then another door opened, and it had a different sound, like the vacuum-sealed closure of a very expensive sedan. A pair of slow, heavy footfalls followed that, along with the slight scent of an aromatic cigar.

Through the receding drug haze, Sage clung to every impression she could, then suddenly, a blinding light shined on her. A body was shoved forward and the light moved from her to Roberto. Men surrounded them as she looked from him to the lights. An older man whose face she could not fully see stood in the shadows smoking a cigar.

"I am so disappointed, Roberto," the old man murmured. "You made me come down from my meetings in Washington, DC, to have this distasteful conversation."

Roberto sprang forward and grabbed her by the throat, toppling the chair as he strangled her.

"How could you do this to me?" he shouted. "You betrayed me! Hector—"

"Betrayed you and is dead," the old man said coolly as three guards wrested Roberto's hands from around Sage's throat and lifted his body away from her.

Gasping and coughing and sucking in dust from the floor, she tried to keep her face away from Roberto's flailing feet. And to think she'd momentarily felt sorry for the bastard.

"Cut her loose," the old man said. "I should enjoy this match. Roberto has caught the tiger by the tail." He took a long drag on his cigar and blew it toward Roberto. "Your problems began with you not honoring me and betraying me . . . and just as the son betrays the father, so the brother betrays the elder brother, and the wife betrays the husband. If you build your house on lies, Roberto, the sin will follow you . . . you should go to church to learn these things. It is God's way."

"My brother is dead," he said in an angry whisper, glaring at Sage as she was released from the chair and stood slowly. "She killed him. He bled to death on the way to the hospital."

"But not before he called me, Roberto—*weeks* ago."

Strangled silence made the Adam's apple bob in Roberto's throat as he strained against the hold of Guzman's men.

"Yes. Believe it. Hector had let me know about this long before we learned of her betrayal . . . which was really the hand of God. You see, I know you, my son. You don't trust unless you verify. I knew you would have her car fitted with a camera, maybe her room, anywhere she might be. So we swept the car and brought your little video back and it produced additional gold."

Roberto's eyes held Sage's as contempt glimmered in them. "Why?"

"Because you killed my family," she said flatly, and then spit on the ground. "You'll never know which ones or remember . . . how many street corners did you spray on your way up? How many innocent people who weren't even involved in your drug trade bled to death on their way to the hospital? How many old women, little kids, young boys . . . Do you even fucking remember!"

"I didn't know those people, and in every war there is collateral damage. I didn't know them, Camille . . . but you *knew* me and I knew you. That is *different*. That is different!"

"Is it?" she said, staring at him as the painful memories flooded back. "Then consider Hector and your business and all of your dreams collateral damage."

"You bitch," Roberto replied through his teeth. "I swear, Camille, you will die before I do this night and then we can both meet in hell."

"Camille isn't even my name," she added in a deadly whisper, leaning toward him and straining against the guards' hold. "You didn't know jack shit, and you most assuredly *never* knew me. Ever . . . and, baby, we already met in hell— each time I tolerated your disgusting touch."

"Let her go," Guzman instructed with a casual wave of his hand, smiling.

The moment the guards released her, she rushed Roberto and punched him in his face hard. "I know I'm going to die tonight, but just let me kick this motherfucker's ass before I do." She stepped back from Roberto and stared at Guzman. "What do you care? He betrayed you, whatever shipment we took down only weakens him, not you—he was coming for you anyway."

"Hell hath no fury . . ." Guzman said, shaking his head. He looked at his men. "What do you think? She is very philosophical, and I like how she thinks. If I thought I could actually convert her to our way of thinking, she would be very useful to our operations on the inside of where she is."

"I'd say let the bastard go and see what she can do," one guard said with an evil grin.

Guzman walked up to Roberto and spat in his face. "You've broken my heart. Your brother is dead and a betrayer. Your money is gone, and your product is burning on the loading docks. Your home in Miami is destroyed, along with all your toys and men who were loyal to you. And now, your woman is DEA and about to fight you in hand-to-hand combat while this house burns to the ground with you both in it . . . and tomorrow is Ash Wednesday. Fitting." Guzman sighed. "Tell me, Roberto. Was it worth it?"

A gunman left the room and ran outside. Immediately Sage smelled the gasoline as he walked around the perimeter of the house. In the distance, chopper blades and sirens disturbed the crickets' songs. When he returned, the others let Roberto go.

For a moment he just stood and looked at her and then suddenly rushed her. She sidestepped him and landed a hard roundhouse kick to his back, much to the delight of the men gathered by the front door. He fell against the small tree and then pushed off from it. That had only enraged him and made him come at her again, this time quickly enough to almost grab hold of her throat again. But anticipating his moves, she reached up and through the small space between them, broke his hold, and made sure her elbow connected hard with his jaw.

Cheering rang out as though a prizefight or a death cage match was underway. But when Roberto fell against one of the guards, he came away with a gun. One shot blew Guzman back. The old man's lit cigar flew over his head and down the steps, igniting the fuel that ripped around the building in a ring of fire. Guards panicked, more concerned about their own safety than seeking retribution for a dead man. Roberto immediately turned the gun on her. And just as quickly a sniper's bullet put him down hard, then in rapidfire succession took out the guards who were trying to flee.

But billowing smoke and heat from fast-moving

flames that ate up soft wood and dry brush now
closed in around her. Windows and doors were
impassable as the inferno raged.

In the chaos, a booming, familiar voice called
her name from above, as she looked up the tree
that was growing up through the floor and out
of the storm-damaged roof. The sound of helicopter blades bore down on her, and she quickly
pulled her body up the rough foliage and through
the small hole in the tarp. She reached up as instructed and a strong hand grabbed hers, then
another hand grabbed her flailing arm, as the
craft pulled up and out of the line of smoke.

Her body collided with metal and sinew as
the chopper moved away from the scene. Jeeps
swarmed the street and the burning house below. Sage closed her eyes and held on tightly to
the only one who'd ever come back for her.

CHAPTER 16

He held her tightly and rocked her as the chopper headed toward NAS, unable to keep up the ruse, not caring that the truth was being witnessed by the small band of brothers who'd flown in and out of hell with him more times than he could count. Lieutenant Hayes simply pounded Lieutenant Butcher's fist with a nod and voiced the single victorious phrase of their brotherhood—*Hoooah.*

If the troubles of the world could just go away now, he would have been a very happy man. But nothing was that simple. There was still a very expensive shipment of some unknown amounts of weaponry, which would be used against American citizens, heading into Canada, based on Sage's DEA intel and what Central Intelligence could piece together from that. Although they'd rounded up his band of merry men, Aalam Bashir, the man Assad reported to, was still at large. Yet it was a solid hunch that he'd be the one to make the weapons ID to initiate the transfer.

The moment they touched down, they all boarded waiting Jeeps and headed to the main admin building. Colonel Mitchell met them, along with Hank Wilson, his core staff, Agent Alvarez, and several key members of Central Intelligence.

Time was of the essence. Everyone who had touched the intersecting cases in any way was now needed to add any intel they could to the joint task force. As they debarked the vehicles and entered the building, all eyes went to Special Agent Sage Wagner and Captain Anthony Davis.

Hank Wilson began clapping long and slow and hard, his meaty palms striking a cadence that contained both respect and clearly personal joy that she was brought home alive. Colonel Mitchell faced Captain Davis, and in a rare display, saluted him indoors.

"Captain, I know this isn't protocol, but I am damned glad to see you."

"Thank you, Colonel," Anthony responded, respectfully. "Wouldn't be here if it wasn't for my men."

"Lieutenants," the colonel said crisply with pride, turning to Anthony's men. "Job well done, but we still have one piece of the puzzle to fit together."

"Sir, if I might interrupt, I also wouldn't be

here and our mission would not have been as successful as it has been so far without the sacrifice and dead-accurate intel provided by Special Agents Sage Wagner and Michael Alvarez. Their DEA team worked seamlessly with ours."

Colonel Mitchell nodded. "We thank you, as does America," he said, looking at both Sage and Mike Alvarez. Then he allowed his gaze to settle on Hank Wilson. "Fine team. I wish all branches of our government worked together the way we did here. Then we could solve a lot of problems. But that's an issue for another day. Right now we still have a piece of the puzzle missing, and I don't want it floating around out there somewhere."

"Thank you," Hank said. "But you're right, Colonel. We're not out of the woods yet." He looked at both of his agents and Sage nodded.

"Guzman said he'd come down from DC just to watch my and Roberto's execution. They are getting really bold and have to have something big planned if a guy like Guzman, at his level, wanted to see me and Roberto burn," Sage said, dragging her fingers through her hair as she stared at the map. "That part just doesn't fit. Pics sent to Colombia should have sufficed."

"Guzman, himself, came to oversee an execution?" Hank looked around the room bewildered.

"He was definitely in the body count Captain Davis and his men left back at that house in the

Ninth Ward when they extracted me, sir," Sage said, and then glanced at Anthony.

"Do you know how high a target of value he was for drug enforcement?" Hank said, bewildered. He looked at the colonel. "He's got assets valued at over a hundred billion and is virtually untouchable—or was."

"This guy Guzman was formerly an unknown to DELTA, but recently came on our radar—not due to his drug affiliations, but because Central Intelligence got photos of him having lunch yesterday with our old Russian nemesis-turned-policy-lobbyist, Dimitri Andropov," Colonel Mitchell said, pushing a folder across the desk at Hank Wilson.

"We've suspected Dimitri of arms dealing for years, but could never prove it," the colonel said in a frustrated tone. "He comes from the old days of the cold war—was one of their generals and also in the intelligence community for that side. Pure KGB. You don't legislate that out of a man. But unless we have hard evidence, we can't keep him out of our backyard. That's the law these days."

"So what is an old arms dealer doing sitting down to lunch at a fine Washington, DC, eatery with a top Colombian drug baron on his way to witness an execution?" Hank ran a palm over his scalp. "Doesn't make sense, but there is a connection we're missing."

"Follow the money," Sage said. "It always comes back to that." She chewed her bottom lip, and paced slowly.

Try as he might to stop himself, he had to watch her move. Anthony's gaze followed Sage's fluid motions and the sexy way she chewed her lip. Every nuance about her was a gift. He was just glad she was alive.

"Assad walked out of the warehouse with five million dollars, a mil from each of the five distributors," Agent Alvarez confirmed as he glanced around. "But here's the deal. Roberto put up five million as a down payment to buy the product from Assad. Half up front to get Assad to put the product on the freighter. Then each distributor brought their cut to the meeting—that's another five, for a total of ten million dollars. The full deal would have been one hundred and fifty million, once we flipped the product. Since Roberto put up half of the investment, he got seventy-five million right off the top. Each of us distributors were supposed to get fifteen million for our one-million-dollar investment—plus there'd be a service fee to Roberto . . . like a mil off the top. But basically it was a crazy-profitable venture."

Lieutenant Butcher released a long whistle. "And you wonder why we can't shut this bull down?"

"But what we confiscated at the docks was only about a million dollars' worth of weapons inventory, if that," the colonel said, glancing around the room.

"What if they are planning on multiple small shipments?" Sage suggested, and then stopped pacing to look at the group. "We know we interrupted five million dollars of potential shipments, because you picked up Assad and his men with that cash right after they left the warehouse. But what happened to the first five million?"

"MI and Central Intelligence report that only a million of it was wire-transferred from the casino to a Mr. Charles Wallace up in Toronto," Colonel Mitchell said.

"There's your payment for what we found on the docks," Anthony replied, glancing at the colonel and then at Sage. "How much you want to bet that the other four million is waiting on the call from Aalam Bashir to Assad to let him know to release the funds."

"But a huge shipment of four million dollars' worth of arms has to come in through a port city. To truck in that much stuff, or to fly it in, or even to bring it in by rail . . . it's possible, but seems like it would be hard to hide—unless it was coming in via multiple small shipments like Agent Wagner said." Alvarez looked around as Anthony turned to the colonel.

"Unless it's nuclear material, sir." Anthony

stepped into the center of the room. "Permission to speak freely?"

"Of course, Captain."

"Thank you, sir. A sighting of Dimitri Andropov with a billionaire drug lord, at this time, is extremely troubling, given what happened in Kazakhstan."

The colonel glanced around the room. "What Captain Davis is about to disclose is highly classified. But we don't have time for clearances and bureaucratic bullshit right now. We need to act before Assad's contact calls him, the payment is perceived as late, or word leaks out that the dock and port have been raided, if it hasn't already. Understood?"

Everyone nodded, and Anthony pressed on. "We lost about a pound of nuclear material during the secret transfer from the Aqtau nuclear plant over there to the UN facility eighteen hundred miles away. There's still debate about whether or not that pound ever existed, if the scales were off, whatever, because we did recover and contain eight hundred pounds. But there's still suspicion that an inside job occurred."

"How does this factor in here, Captain?" Hank Wilson asked, clearly troubled. "It don't get how this fits with Colombian drug dealers at all. This is way out of Guzman's normal span of control or interest."

Anthony nodded. "Hear me out, sir. This is pure speculation, but what if Assad's terror cell was only spending half the money—since they'd only set up wire transfers for half? That five million in cash they physically carried away from the warehouses could go back to fund other aspects of their cell's operations, and they just purchased a million dollars in conventional weapons. But then they also may have purchased something special that's worth four million dollars . . . and that's small, light, and easy to transport—something that is our worst fear."

"If we can crack the code on who this Charles Wallace really is, the guy who the wire transfers were sent to, then maybe we can figure out if this guy has the capacity to deliver something like that to Bashir?" Sage added.

"We've been running that name through the MI databases to no avail," the colonel admitted, and then smoothed a palm over his head.

"A lot of loose nukes got away from Mother Russia," Sage replied, casting her gaze around the room. "What was Dimitri Andropov doing meeting with Guzman? It still comes back to that." She looked at her boss. "Anybody keeping tabs on his whereabouts now?"

Colonel Mitchell looked at the Central Intelligence staff in the room, and one of their agents who sat before a laptop pulled up a screen.

"Andropov left DC on a morning flight to attend a technology conference in Boston, sir."

"Check all the charter flights leaving from Boston to Toronto and any passenger manifests with a Charles Wallace on them." Sage leaned against the wall and looked at Anthony. "How's your Arabic, Captain?"

"Never better."

"We can run Captain Davis's voice through a voice synthesizer and make him sound like Assad, if he keeps his communication short and sweet," the staffer from Central Intelligence said. "We can record key words and phrases and answer in bursts to satisfy the caller without Captain Davis even having to be in the room."

"Meanwhile, we can get a DELTA team up there in Toronto to—"

"Wait, wait, wait!" Sage said waving her arms and cutting off the colonel mid-sentence. "Please forgive me, sir, but it's coming together in my head!" She walked back and forth quickly. "Guzman knew Roberto was betraying him by doing a deal with Assad behind his back—long before he found out about me. He said so in that shack. Guzman was toying with Roberto. It was even Guzman's men that swept the red Mercedes to get video of me calling in for support from my DEA team. Roberto wouldn't have enough juice to broker an arms deal for Assad . . . he got *played* by the old men! Guzman also said something about Ash Wednesday, which sounds really strange. It was out of context, like the old fox knew something else Roberto didn't."

Sage walked back and forth in front of the group. "Any arms transactions coming from Uzbekistan on a freighter—that's gotta be your boy Dimitri, Colonel. He can put a nice Anglo name on it, but of course Dimitri would want his money wired to Canada and then to a Swiss or Cayman account. If it went to Canada first, that transfer wouldn't be an immediate red flag in the casino's system. Then coming out of an international businessman's account in Canada to anywhere doesn't seem so suspicious. Also, if I wanted to move something small and radioactive, I'd bring it on a train!"

"Damn, Wagner. That's so obvious, now that you say it." Hank rubbed his palms down his face. "During Mardi Gras, it's impossible to move around New Orleans by car, right. Airports have heightened security, and by boat is too slow. But if I wanted to get something real bad out of this country, I'd ride the rails all the way to Houston and take a cruise to Mexico."

"That's just the thing," Anthony said to Hank Wilson. "These guys aren't necessarily interested in getting a pound of bomb-making materials *out* of the United States. That's just where they'd want them to be. They had plans for physically moving the conventional weapons—which we interrupted."

Sage stared at him now. "Washington, DC." She covered her mouth for a moment as the room fell quiet. "If you had an old buddy who had offices and did lunch with congressmen and senators, wouldn't you visit him in DC and tell him that DC might not be the place to be on All Saints Day . . . like the day after Mardi Gras? A calendar date that might also have significance to fundamentalist extremists?"

"*Ash* Wednesday," Anthony said and closed his eyes. "Damn."

"And if you knew his young protégé had scratched your money itch," Sage pressed on, "might you not encourage your old friend to go visit New Orleans where you knew it would be safe . . . a place where he could also take back the business that was stolen after that errant protégé was duly punished? This keeps an old balance of power, an old friendship intact, while Andropov gets to sell weapons to Al Qaeda."

"And at a technology fair in Boston, it would be easy to pick up a strange contraption and get on the train with it headed to DC," Colonel Mitchell said. "I want every unit we have stateside combing trains from Boston to DC." He looked at Central Intelligence wild-eyed. "Shut down the goddamned northeast corridor rail system if you have to!"

"But, sir," Anthony interjected. "While I agree the threat has a very high probability of moving on the rail system, Aalam Bashir is not about to blow himself up. Top members of the terror cells leave that to peasants. We need to get images from Central Intelligence to track who Aalam Bashir met with while he was potentially in Boston."

"We can scan for him," one of the intelligence staffers said. "We'll start with high probability border crossing areas . . . Since we have Toronto as one of them, let's see if we can place him at the conference under a different name—or back into finding him by using Andropov's photo as a locator."

"Good, make it so," the colonel said, still focused on Anthony. "So, Captain, talk to us. What's your hunch from there?"

"During Mardi Gras, all transportation hubs are a madhouse." Anthony went to the map on the whiteboard and drew a line with his finger. "If I were a terrorist who wasn't going to blow myself up, I'd hand off my package in a train station—I'd send my suicide bomber to DC from Boston, which is only a six-and-a-half-hour run . . . but I'd go from Boston to New Orleans by rail myself to take advantage of being able to board with the cover of a technology conference and debark where it was chaotic. My face would be more recognizable than some unknown person I'd talked into the twenty-one virgins deal."

Pausing to think for a moment, Anthony rubbed the nape of his neck and spoke with a frown. "So I'd need the extra cover of a crowd and I'd go to meet my men with the money, while some poor sucker nuked DC. The trigger to send Charles Wallace his cash is if that nuke actually works and detonates—not just having obtained some product from the old Soviet Republic that may or may not be worth squat. For that much money for a pound of product, I'd need to see or read about a mushroom cloud. The call Assad and his men are waiting on is to connect with Aalam Bashir in the New Orleans train station and to bring the cash . . . on a day when it's virtually impossible for train authorities to spot-check people due to overwhelming crowds."

"When Bashir calls his men here in New Orleans, we can answer . . . and we can maybe stall, claiming traffic problems," Sage said, sounding unsure. "But they should already have his train schedule. They should already be there in the station to meet him."

"If Aalam was going to get here tonight from Boston, he'd have to have gotten on a train yesterday morning at eight fifteen A.M.," an intelligence staffer said. "That would put him in New Orleans at seven thirty-eight P.M. tonight."

Everyone looked at their watches.

Sage looked at Anthony. "That's less than a half hour from now."

CHAPTER 17

Sage jogged next to an intelligence agent who handed her a large shoulder purse filled with a gun, cell phone, lipstick, and a compact. By the time she debarked from the chopper, she would have to look like a regular civilian, not someone who'd been in a firefight. The female agent had given her a new sweater by simply stripping off her own and trading right there in the situation room, and they'd gotten the dirt off her face while Anthony quickly recorded key words and phrases.

All agreed that a military presence in the train station might spook Bashir and they stood a chance of either losing him or having him tell his man in DC to detonate immediately. But a couple coming to meet family for the Big Easy festivities wouldn't gain notice. This wasn't about a show of force, but finesse—her ballgame.

They'd have to apprehend this rat bastard in

the middle of hundreds of innocent civilians, so it wasn't about storming the train station or having a huge shoot-out. They'd have to take Bashir down nice and easy. But first they'd have to get there on time.

Their chopper set down in the US Post Office lot over on Loyola and Girod, but that meant a two-block run past Julia Street to Howard Avenue. The prayer was that Bashir didn't do what most folks did, call a few minutes before the train entered the station to give the person waiting the heads-up to be there. But if he did, they were ready. Intelligence had rigged Anthony's cell to bounce the signal to them, his response would go through their voice synthesizer, then to the caller. It was the only way to get ambient train station sound—but if Bashir called while they were in the chopper, their plan was cooked.

As soon as they debarked, they began running. DEA would support with agents in plainclothes looking like holiday revelers, DELTA units would be hidden and guarding the perimeter, but she and Anthony had to flush and apprehend the target.

She grabbed his hand as they entered the train station and squeezed hard. "Slow down and smile. You look tense, like you're hunting somebody."

He nodded, slowing his breathing by inhaling deeply through his nose. "What if I'm wrong?

What if this was all speculation and something really bad is moving on a ship or a cargo—"

She kissed him hard and then backed off.

"What was that for?" he said quietly.

"You're not wrong and you need a reason to be breathing hard." She smiled at him and glanced over his shoulder. "The train is dumping passengers. You need to look really casual. We'll know in a minute if our theory is wrong."

He kissed her hard.

"What was that for?" she said, smiling.

"For not dying on me, Sage Wagner."

But she didn't have time to respond. From her peripheral vision she saw a man that closely matched Bashir's description melt into the throng and press a cell phone to his ear. When Anthony's phone sounded, they parted. She headed for Bashir, Anthony moved through the crowd to stay on the flush side of the trap.

"*Assalamu Alaikum,*" Anthony said, as Sage pushed through the crowd.

Moving like an NFL linebacker, Sage put her shoulder down, barely excusing herself as she pushed through to Bashir and then hugged him.

"Uncle! You made it," she shrieked loud enough for Anthony as well as Intelligence to hear her through the phone.

"Unhand me, Miss!" Bashir shouted, and then cursed as he dropped the cell phone.

Pretending to be clueless, she acted like she

was trying to retrieve it and kicked it away under an oblivious human throng.

"I'll get it, Uncle," she said, holding his arm. "Where's Auntie? How was the train ride, long I bet?"

Bashir pushed her away with both hands. "I do not know who you are, you crazy person! You have mistaken me, I assure you!"

Cold steel met the base of Bashir's skull as civilians suddenly screamed.

"No, we're not mistaken," Anthony said in a low, threatening tone. "And the only reason you're still alive is because these good people don't need to see your head blown off."

EPILOGUE

Six Weeks Later . . . Chicago, Illinois . . .

Six weeks was no time and yet a long time for a man to contemplate his entire future. If DELTA hadn't been able to identify and take down Bashir's hand-off man when the train stopped in New York en route to DC, there might not have been a future for millions of innocent people. And yet, having Sage in his arms made him know how much he'd been living like a man who had no future, only a painful past, only a hard present, without anything to look forward to.

She was what he looked forward to . . . and it took six weeks of bureaucracy and After Action Report paperwork on both her side and his to get free for a few weeks. Plus there was his promotion and hers. It was the hardest six weeks he'd ever had to endure . . . waiting for her, and now she was doing her woman thing—freshening up. Whatever that meant. Making him wait a few more excruciating minutes until she came back into the bedroom.

But what she'd never understand as a woman was this—he would have loved her right there in an airport bathroom or out behind the burning shack in the Ninth Ward, for all he cared. But she cared, so it mattered to him. He just wanted to be with her and to never be without her again.

She'd called him her hero when the madness was all over, but didn't she know every so-called hero needed a national anthem? That's what she was for him, that one intangible thing that made a man believe in something greater than himself, made him salute, made him stand up with his hand over his heart and pledge his allegiance to it . . . to her. Something . . . someone worth dying for, if necessary.

The soft R&B playing on his docked iPod had been selected just for her; the song masters crooned the truth of how he felt so much more eloquently than he could have ever delivered it. And the truth was, he didn't want to be sitting on the edge of the bed in the W hotel waiting for her—he wanted to be in their home. Somewhere permanent.

As he looked at the bathroom door, waiting for it to open, waiting for an angel to appear from behind it, he knew he'd made the right decision. He'd kept his family's home in Bronzeville, renting it out . . . hell, he was always on the go. Now it was worth a mint. He'd banked the insurance payments from his father's, brother's, and finally his mother's passing. All of it eventually rolled down to him and he'd bought properties in Hyde Park way back when.

But for some odd reason, on their first time back together and her first visit to Chicago, he wanted to not only show Sage the tourist attractions, but also where he'd played blacktop basketball, gone to school . . . wanted her to see the roots he had or maybe hold his hand as he rediscovered them for himself. Maybe a little of both.

Nostalgia claimed him as he waited for her. He'd lived like a nomad and didn't use much of his salary, never thinking he'd live this long, just socked it away. If she wanted to build a home . . . yeah, he could do that. If she wanted a building for a rec center to give kids alternatives and a positive place to be, yeah, he could fight the war on drugs at home with her—could fight it by turning around one kid at a time. She just had to say the word.

Or he could stay in the military and advance his career in noncombat positions, if he elected to, after this last tour of duty put him on the map, or as an officer he could retire at will with thirty days' notice. But she didn't have to go back to what had almost crushed her soul. The choice was hers, he'd just facilitate that decision.

She'd made him think about all of that with her smile and her laughter over the phone. Had made the bottom drop out of his stomach when he saw her again in the airport for the first time. Made him wish he could breach civilian airspace and fly a chopper from O'Hare to the W, instead of driving an hour into town with her hand resting on his knee giving him wood.

He'd been daydreaming so hard that when the bathroom door suddenly opened, it startled him enough to make him stand. She laughed and shook her head.

"Isn't this how we began, Major?" She walked over to him slowly and fit her body against his. "Me catching you unawares?"

He couldn't even smile or return her teasing now. He'd wanted her so badly for so long . . . There was minimal blood flow to his brain at the moment. The only way he knew to tell her what she meant to him was through touch . . . to become delirious in the fragrant scent of her silky brown hair, nuzzling her neck and planting heat-filled kisses against her satin smooth skin until she gasped. Finding the small dimples in her lower back, paying them homage with his thumbs beneath her soft, cashmere sweater just before he palmed her exquisite ass and drew her to him harder . . . that's how he would let her know.

He was a man of action, not a man of many words. No, he couldn't play with her or tease her right now. For him, this was no game. It had become as real as it could get. And when her breathing changed, he knew she knew that too.

Her touch went from gentle caresses to a more urgent tug against his sweater. That was all he needed to feel to make him strip the garment up over his head. What started out as her request became her direct order. No words were exchanged, just her touch and her hitched breathing when she felt the burn of his torso. She pulled off her sweater and allowed it to hit the floor, then saved him the trouble of having to fight with her black lace bra. Hands behind her, she unhooked it. His palms caught the bounty when it fell away, and he moaned with her, savoring her ripe lobes of flesh.

Piece by piece, shoes and jeans and boxers and lace fell to the floor. Third-degree skin-on-skin contact caused hissing air to be sucked in through clenched teeth. Kisses wild, wet, and deep, became whale song moans submerged in open-mouth chasms. His hands begged her forgiveness for taking so long to get back to this, to get back to her, for being deployed, for having to be anywhere other than here. And her body told him that it didn't matter what words hadn't been spoken as he fell back with her on his lap. His apology was accepted as it slid into her hot, slick sheath on her wail.

God knows, this time he'd been prepared. The

box was right on the nightstand so she could see that he wasn't playing. But she wasn't hearing it, wasn't playing with him either at all this time. To be sure he was clear about her intent, she rode him hard where he sat on the edge of the bed, arching his back as she held on to his neck, burying his face against her breasts . . . begging his pardon for not being able to tease him or wait for him to reach across the king-size bed.

Each pull back into her heaven practically made him stand with her still on his lap. Muscles corded in his thighs, back, and neck. His arms trembled not from lifting her, but from the pleasure rushing through every limb. Wet friction heat skin-slapped him senseless; he could hear it keeping time with his heartbeat and the throb in his shaft.

Burning Sage purified him on the white-on-white duvet, became a shaman's spirit walk, a pilgrim's journey, ecstasy and religious experience no respecter of age or gender. He cried out, wept, held on to her body unable to stop. Her hair became his private confessional for all that he'd done in uniform and out, as he filled his hands with it, buried his face against it, whispered "I love you" into it . . . Absolution came from her as a chant of his name, devolving from Anthony to Tony to T . . . then a shrieked *papi* . . .

It was that last mea culpa that broke him, that dropped the bottom out of his scrotum and offered her name up in baritone breath segments, seed pulsing from his body in waves of combined pleasure and pain.

He sat on the edge of the bed with her on his lap, held tightly in his arms, panting. This was so not how he'd planned it. He was going to be cool, take his time, do the damned thing right . . . taste her, touch her, drive her crazy all weekend.

"I've never experienced anything like this in my life," she murmured against his neck, still breathing hard and then broke down in tears.

Truth be told, neither had he—not where he wanted to plant some seed, make a baby, and put down roots.

He rocked her and held her, not sure what to do, not having any frame of reference for handling a woman's tears, especially when she was naked and trembling and still sheathing him.

After a few minutes he sought her mouth and wiped her cheeks, then kissed away where the tears had been. "I want to show you who I am and what you mean to me, okay?"

She bit her lip with tears still shimmered in her gorgeous brown eyes. "Okay."

"But we have to get dressed."

"Really? Now?"

The way she'd said it made him smile. It was just four o'clock in the afternoon, and they'd been in the room maybe forty-five minutes tops. What had just happened was hot and frenetic, the same way they'd met . . . but he had an important mission that he now knew couldn't wait.

"Yeah," he murmured, standing with her legs wrapped around his waist. "Gotta take a shower and get dressed, because I have something really important to show you."

As they laughed together, he carried her into the bathroom, sat on the edge of the tub, and turned on the water and adjusted the temperature, then cut on the shower. When she tried to climb off him, he shook his head, making her laugh harder.

"Don't get my hair wet, then," she squealed as he gave the spray his back.

"You lather . . . I'll scrub."

Damn, he loved the W's wide showers. She did add soap and *Hoooah*, he damned sure made it lather. But she'd turned around all his plans, had changed everything he was gonna do . . . now he knew what it was that would best explain what she meant to him. A dinner and a candlelit evening was too cliché. That wasn't how they'd met. The bottom had dropped out for both of them. She needed to know how much it had for him, that he'd never recovered and was still free-falling.

Sage took her time tracing his back as she dried it with a thick towel and then just let it fall to the floor. She knew he had something to show her burning inside him, but he was all she really wanted.

Didn't the man understand that they'd made it out alive? He'd made it home from all his tours of duty and this most crazy one yet. That was all she needed to see of Chicago, but because whatever this thing was that he wanted to show her was important to him, it was important to her.

Yet the heat that he'd planted between her legs wouldn't go away. Dark copper bronze skin glistened under her hands and she couldn't stop pelting it with reverent kisses until he moaned. Dropping the towel, she let the bathroom steam cloak them in a humid blanket, tracing the thick cords of muscle in his back, across his broad shoulders and down his tightly ridged biceps.

"If you keep that up, we'll never get out of this room," he murmured as her cheek rested against his back and her hands slowly splayed against his chest, then trailed down the hard bricks in his abdomen to his groin.

"I can't help it," she murmured, telling the truth with her words and her touch. "I love the way you feel as much as I love the way you make me feel . . . and I've missed you so much."

When he turned around and kissed her, then slid down her body, she backed up against the sink and braced herself on her palms, almost afraid she'd pass out.

"If you do that," she murmured hoarsely, "we definitely won't get out of this room."

Ignoring her, he ran his hand up her leg and lifted it to hook it over his shoulder. "I'll take my chances," he murmured against her bud, teasing it with the mere vibration of his voice. He spoke to her there, as though that part of her had a mind of its own, which for him it did. "You told me I could take the hill . . . the beach . . . plant a flag . . . didn't you say that the first night we knew this was real?"

Head back, eyes closed, the only answer was the elongated truth, "Yessss . . ."

He kissed her deeply, gently suckling the tender flesh. "Then let me take the beach before we go out . . ."

There was no defense against this man of DELTA Force. He'd captured her mind, owned her heart, and was conquering her body one sweet tongue flick at a time. If it was his mission to take the beach, then mission accomplished, as her head lolled back and her breaths became staccato surrender.

Pleasure built in a slow, undulating wave that crested higher and higher, now blending her voice into the surrendered breaths, making her grip tighten along the edge of the marble, making her body ebb and flow with his rolling tongue until her sanity came crashing down and washed against his face.

Breathless, she leaned so far back her head rested against the bathroom mirror. He smiled up at her, wiped his face with a discarded towel, and then kissed his way up her belly to claim her mouth.

Gathering her in his arms, he attempted to get out of the bathroom, but made the strategic mistake of allowing his hot shaft to rest against her. The heat of it demanded attention, even though he tried to act like it didn't. His moan gave him away as she slipped him inside her, and his body buckled with the shudder that erupted from her. For a moment they just had to cling to each other as the intense pleasure event passed through them, his forehead resting against hers before he started moving.

"I can't get enough of you," he whispered, thrusting slowly.

"And that's a problem how?" she murmured and then gasped as he began to pump harder, sliding his hands between her ass and the smooth marble.

"Because I have something I've gotta show you . . . outside . . . before it gets too late."

"Okay," she whispered. "Just . . . this . . . last . . . time—then we can go, baby."

"All right," he said against her damp hair, lifting her up under the stretched lobes of her ass and walking her back into the bedroom. "Just . . . this . . . last . . . time."

* * *

The only way to get out of the room two hours later was for each of them to go into the bathroom alone, shower, and dress in the bathroom. It was beyond ridiculous.

He dragged her by the hand through the lobby with damp hair and her scarf half falling off, and they laughed as they got in a cab at the curb. Knowing she would object and try to eavesdrop, he told her to cover her ears while he leaned forward and quietly gave the cabbie the address.

"No . . . it'll ruin the surprise," he said laughing and loving her kisses and light shoves. "You can't break this soldier. Name, rank, and serial number only."

"But . . ."

He stopped her questions with deep kisses the entire way, not caring if the cabbie watched his very public display of affection. If the man told him to get a room, he was in such a good mood that he'd tell him he already had one—but was on a mission.

They got out at 233 S. Wacker Drive. Amusement filled him as he paid the man and watched Sage survey the street with a frown of confusion, her eyes canvassing the downtown area. She never looked up. Perfect.

He caught her hand and moved her toward the destination building with a tug; that's when she gasped and threw her head back and laughed.

"The Willis Tower! Oh my God! I always wanted to do that!"

Pleased, he just shrugged, trying not to allow her squeal to run all through him too badly in public. "It used to be named the Sears Tower . . . so I figured this was as good a place as any to visit. We had aliases, this is now different, and . . . you know . . . I guess we're different."

She didn't say a word, just kissed him and leaned against him as they entered the building and got a ticket on the 103rd floor. His stomach was in knots the entire way up, but he hoped that she'd never know that. And of course, there was a wait . . . until he went to the admissions attendant and whispered in the woman's ear.

The older woman beamed at him and then hugged him, and then held him back to look up at him. "My son was in the service and I wish he could do this. So I'm letting you to the front of the line. Thank you for what you do for our country."

"Thank you, ma'am, I can't tell you how much I really appreciate this."

"No, we appreciate *you*." She then spoke loudly to the throngs that had been waiting. "This man is a DELTA Force veteran—let him through, folks. He's home on leave and got his sweetie visiting Chi-town . . . now y'all step aside."

To his surprise, there were no sulking glances or murmuring comments. People stepped aside for him and Sage, stood taller, and an older man in the group began the applause. Sage hesitated, clearly not wanting to put people out, but the good nature of the crowd spurred her onward.

"C'mon," he said quietly. "We won't hold up the groups for long. I just wanted you to see my city from a thousand or so feet off the ground."

He loved her smile and her giggle as she stepped out into the clear Plexiglas enclosure, looked down for a second, and then squeezed her eyes shut.

"Oh my God, Anthony! Get me out of here! Okay, okay, I did it. I'm getting dizzy!"

It was clear from the laughter behind them and the way people were craning their necks that, a private confessional was out of the question. So he held her hand tightly and dropped to one knee, not knowing the exact words to say. But the older ladies behind him were in his amen corner, squealing and swooning before he could even form the words he wanted to give just to Sage.

"I brought you up here," he said, looking up at Sage and holding her hand. "Because this is how you make me feel . . . like I'm on top of the world, but the bottom is dropping out from under me all at the same time. Pure vertigo. And . . . I hope I make you feel like that, too . . . just a little bit. I've been all over the world, but never felt like I could be home or was home, until I met you. So I know I didn't say all I could about what you mean to me, but . . . Sage Wagner, will you marry me?"

He never heard her answer as the crowd erupted in a spontaneous cheer behind them. Kids started a stadium wave as Sage nodded profusely and started crying. He dug into the pocket of his leather jacket for the thing that had been burning a hole in it since he'd picked her up at the airport.

All of his fingers felt like thumbs as he extracted the small velvet case and popped the top, praying to God that three karats would be big enough and that she liked the oval shape surrounded by a cluster of tiny diamonds.

Trying not to drop it, he slid the ring on her slender finger and kissed the back of her hand, and then watched her slide down to the Plexiglas floor to kiss him long and slow and deep before a cheering crowd. That's when he knew his mission was accomplished.

They had a room and he could show her the rest of Chicago tomorrow.